HOOCH AND HOWLS

AN EBB & FLOW PREQUEL

Karenna Colcroft

This book is a work of fiction. Names, characters, places, and incidents either are products of the author's imagination or are used fictitiously. Any resemblance to actual events or locales or persons, living or dead, is entirely coincidental.

Warnings: This book includes a scene in which the main character spies, without consent, on two people having sex. It also contains references to past sexual assault and underage male prostitution.

Published by

Vegan Wolf Productions

veganwolfproductions@gmail.com

Cover Art by Kim Ramsey-Winkler

NO AI WAS USED IN THE CREATION OF THIS STORY OR ITS COVER.

A BRIEF GUIDE TO KARENNA'S UNIVERSE

A LITTLE ABOUT WEREWOLVES

- Werewolves are made, not born. A person becomes a werewolf when an attack by a werewolf is so severe that the person almost dies. The new werewolf remains unconscious for 1-3 days in wolf form while their newly-acquired healing ability repairs the damage to their body.
- On the night of the full moon, werewolves have to shift into wolf form for several hours. During the rest of the month, they can shift if and when they choose to.
- Werewolves have an innate healing ability that can repair almost any injury. The only exceptions are rapid blood loss or injuries inflicted by a silver bullet. This healing ability slows the aging process. Werewolves can live for over 200 years, though around the 200-year mark, they often develop dementia.
- Werewolves have vastly heightened senses, especially hearing and smell. Often, when changed, they acquire a new gift such as reading minds or predicting the future.
- Werewolves typically live in packs, though some choose to live as lone wolves. There are also werewolves who are ordered to live packless as punishment for a crime.
- Uterus-having werewolves can't bear children because the fetus won't survive shifting forms. Sperm-producing werewolves sometimes choose to father children with humans. The child of a werewolf is always human.
- There are only a few death-penalty crimes in the werewolf world: Killing, while in wolf form, a human or a werewolf who is in human form; changing someone who is under the age of 18; or deliberately revealing the existence of werewolves to humans without first obtaining permission from a leader.
- Werewolves who are partnered/married to humans or who have children can request permission to tell those family members that they're a werewolf. Other exceptions

are made on a case-by-case basis. The human world at large does not know werewolves exist, and the humans who do know are sworn to secrecy.

- Compulsion, or compelling, is a gift that werewolves obtain when they reach a leadership rank, though some werewolves have it as their innate gift. A werewolf who has the power of compulsion can give commands to other werewolves and sometimes humans, and the others are unable to disobey.
- Werewolves rise through ranks in one of two ways: By fighting and defeating the wolf who is ranked immediately above them or by succession if a wolf leaves the pack or dies.
- Werewolves are expected to have permission to enter any pack territory other than their own.

THE WORLD'S ARRANGEMENT

- Each country has its own werewolf ruler. Once a year, each country's ruler hosts the leaders of every pack, and every region if applicable, in the country.
- Geographically larger countries, such as the United States and Canada, are broken into regions that encompass the territories of multiple packs. In addition to the national ruler, each region has a leader. Twice a year, regional leaders host the leaders of every pack in the region.
- In the United States, Alaska and Hawaii are each their own region. All U.S. territories are encompassed by a single region. There are ten additional U.S. regions, each of which encompasses several states.
- In Canada, the provinces of New Brunswick, Nova Scotia, and Prince Edward Island form the Maritimes Region. Each of the other provinces, and each of the Canadian territories, is its own region due to geographic size.

HONORIFICS

In my universe, there are five titled ranks among werewolves, along with two pack roles that aren't titled but are held in high esteem in most packs and one honorific that can apply to any other werewolf. They are:

Anax: The ruler of all werewolves within a given country

Arkhon: The ruler of a region within a country

Alpha: The leader of an individual pack

Beta: Second-in-command of an individual pack; takes over if the Alpha is away or incapacitated

Peacekeeper: Third-in-command of an individual pack; their job is to maintain peace within the pack and peace between their pack and others.

Healer: A healer is a werewolf who is able to use their innate healing ability to heal others as well as themself. A healer might hold any rank within their pack, and some alphas declare their healer to be outside of pack hierarchy to ensure that the healer isn't injured or killed in a challenge fight.

Tracker: Trackers are essentially a pack's police force. Any member of a pack can become a tracker by choice or by being asked by pack leadership to assume the role. The tracker with the highest pack rank becomes head tracker.

"Old friend": This is an honorific primarily used by the highest-ranked werewolves when speaking to another leader or someone from another pack to indicate that they consider the other person an ally and are willing to work in cooperation with them. It is used regardless of how long the werewolves in question have actually known each other.

CHAPTER ONE

THE SILENCE was deafening. Living alone, Malachi had grown accustomed to silence, but occasionally it became too much for him. This was one of those times. The walls seemed to close around him. His inner wolf clamored for freedom. It was time to run.

The moment he stepped out of the cottage, Malachi smelled them. Humans. In his territory. At this time of year, they had no business here, but the scent was unmistakable.

"Blast." He stood in the doorway for a moment, unable to choose whether to go back in or go outside as he'd planned. He couldn't run if there were humans nearby. Too many questions would arise if anyone saw a wolf here on Herman's Island.

The thought of going back into the cottage nauseated him. For two weeks, he'd left the building only in the early mornings, and then only for brief periods. For a werewolf, staying indoors was no better than being caged, but it was preferable to the pack finding him. This place had been his home for over a decade, and now it belonged to him legally since his parents had drowned in a boating accident the previous summer. They'd left him everything despite not having seen him in years. They'd known only that their strange, moody son had gone to university in Halifax and had never returned.

They hadn't known about the night he'd brought a girl—his

fiancée, although he hadn't yet told his parents about the engagement—to the cottage. They'd never learned about the attack that had left the girl dead, her throat ripped out. Malachi had survived out of sheer Irish will, as his father would have put it. He'd survived to take revenge on the wolf who had changed him and killed the girl he loved.

That wolf's pack, Mahone Bay, based nearby, had tried to take Malachi in, but he had refused. He'd stayed with them only long enough to kill his attacker and learn a few of the rules that governed shifters. He wasn't the joining kind. Instead he'd taken to the woods of this island during the months when the summer cottages remained vacant. In summer, he stayed indoors as much as he could or rowed out to hide from the humans on one of the smaller, unpopulated islands that dotted the bay.

Sometimes other wolves had come, and he'd chased them off or fought them, depending on how unwilling they were to leave when told. He'd yet to lose a fight, and since word had spread that he would defend his small territory, most wolves who chanced upon him left without incident.

The last one, though, had been very resistant, and Malachi had killed him, not knowing at the time that the strange wolf held a high rank in another nearby pack. He'd learned of his error the following day, when members of that pack and Mahone Bay came looking for the stranger. Fearing retribution, Malachi had chosen to hide.

This was his first venture outside after dawn since then, other than to bring in firewood from the stack beside the cottage, and now he couldn't have the run he so desperately needed because there were fucking humans in his territory. Hiding his nature from humans was one of the few werewolf laws he chose to obey. Even if they didn't see him shift, spotting a wolf here would certainly rouse their suspicion.

To hell with them. He didn't fear humans, only the possibility that they might find out what he was. He could play the role of angry landowner and chase them off.

Choosing to stay in human form for the moment, he moved almost silently through the undergrowth and trees that grew a few yards from the cottage. A slight breeze blew uphill from the water, and Malachi's heightened sense of smell told him he would find the intruders on the beach. He angled his path in that direction. Before long, he heard the humans' voices.

"Ain't we supposed to meet them in town?" The young male voice trembled slightly. "If we don't show up on time, they'll kill us."

"They'd have to find us first." This male sounded more confident and a bit older than the first speaker. "Relax, Jonny. We have time for some fun before we meet them."

"This isn't fun. It's cold out here, Roger. I just want to get to town and drop off the shipment. If anyone found us…" He didn't finish his sentence.

"No one's going to find us. Relax." Roger's voice was low and persuasive, almost seductive.

Malachi's lip curled. He didn't care if men fucked other men, but he didn't want to see it on his beach. And the men below seemed to be heading that way. He took a few more steps and stopped short when the younger man said, "Wait. I hear something."

"You're imagining things," Roger said impatiently. "Quit stalling. You know why I let you come with me, Jonathan. You made the promise without even being asked. No one's around here. No more excuses."

"I—I can't. What if someone sees? What if it hurts?"

Slowly, taking even more care to be silent, Malachi moved forward. Now he could see the men on the beach below. A rowboat with a large wooden crate inside was pulled up onto the sand, and beside it stood the men, one blond and scrawny, barely more than a boy; the other a few inches taller than his companion, with sun-weathered skin and dark hair.

The dark man's hand encircled the blond's arm. "You can. You said you want to. Might hurt a bit, but I'll be careful."

Malachi growled. While he had little use for humans, the younger was obviously reluctant. He refused to allow the man to be manipulated like this.

“Please,” Jonathan whimpered. “I haven’t—I can’t, Roger. I just can’t. I’m too scared.”

“Fucking hell.” Roger shoved him away and stalked to the rowboat. “This’ll relax you if nothing else will. There’s nothing to be scared of. You know I’d never hurt you. Just first-time jitters, that’s all you have.”

The younger man’s face went white. “They’ll kill us if anything’s missing!”

“They’ll never know. We nail the cover back in place and they’ll think the shipment was just short. Shut up if you’re so afraid someone’s here. They won’t find us if we’re quiet.”

He picked up a large, flat rock from the ground and used it to pry open the crate. Malachi crouched in the bushes, waiting for the right moment to intervene. The younger man’s fear spiced the breeze, and Malachi couldn’t stand by and let him be victimized.

Roger took a large jug from the crate and held it up. “Here. Have some of this and you won’t worry about a thing.”

He opened the jug. The pungent scent of strong booze joined the other smells on the wind.

Malachi tensed. These men were bootleggers, that much was clear, and the cargo they carried surely wasn’t intended for one to use to coerce the other.

Roger shoved the jug at Jonathan, who stepped back. The hooch spilled over the sand, its smell, uncontained by the jug, so strong Malachi could taste it. It intoxicated him. He’d never been a drinking man, and this was why. Alcohol heavily affected him, even its fumes. It took away his reason. Even before his change, it had been so. Now, senses heightened by the wolf, he had no hope of avoiding the hooch’s effects.

Clinging desperately to his shreds of rational thought, he forced himself to remain hidden. The men no doubt believed themselves alone. He had no place here.

“Here, Jonny!” Roger took a swig from the jug and held it out again. “Don’t waste it, blast you. It’ll help ease things. You promised me. I know you keep your word.”

"I..." The blond took the jug and raised it. He was attractive, no doubt about it, and the sight of his lips around the neck of the jug brought images to Malachi's mind of those lips around something else. They did nothing to improve his self-control.

Perhaps he didn't have to control himself. They were on his beach, already preparing to fuck. There was no reason he couldn't join them.

That's the hooch talking, the rational part of his brain told him.

Then shut up and let me listen.

He crouched lower to the ground, not wanting the men to see him quite yet. In his younger years, he had refused to accept his attraction to men. He was expected to want women, and so he had forced that to be the case. Now there was no one to judge him for his desires, or for acting on them if he chose. These men certainly couldn't judge.

He would judge himself, though. If not for indulging with men, for doing so without invitation. Alcohol lowered his inhibitions, but he would not allow it to take away his morals. If invited, he would sate his need with these men. Otherwise, he would take matters into his own hands, quite literally. There was no excuse for force or coercion when one could relieve one's own lust.

Of course, his hand was nowhere near as appealing as the pale, slim-fingered hand of the blond. Or the rougher-looking hand of the dark-haired man.

Enough. Malachi growled again, low in his throat so he wouldn't be heard. He wanted the humans gone.

He wanted the humans.

He touched his hard shaft through his trousers. Since taking up residence in the cottage, he had avoided humans and werewolves alike. He had become celibate, running instead of fucking when frustration and desire grew too strong.

Clearly his celibacy was by circumstance, not preference. He wanted to fuck. The animal side of him and the human side both. The hooch added to his lust, but it wasn't the only cause.

"I—I think I can try now, Roger," the blond said hesitantly.

"Take down your trousers, then," Roger said hoarsely. "Fuck, Jonathan, don't make me wait anymore. Give me what you said is mine or I'll take it." He held up his hand. "No. I won't take you by force, Jonny. Don't fear. I swore I'd not do that to you. But you swore you'd allow me."

"Please." Even from a distance, fear and arousal rose from the blond man in equal waves. Malachi hadn't detected the arousal before. "Why here, Roger? Why now?"

"Because I say so." The taller man grabbed the waist of the blond's trousers and yanked him toward him. "'Help me, Roger. I need money, Roger. I have nowhere to go, Roger. I'll give you anything you like if you help me.' Does that sound familiar?"

"Y—yes."

Malachi bristled as he saw the younger man tremble, but again his senses told him that fear wasn't the only emotion there. Jonathan wasn't afraid of Roger, but rather of his own desires. Malachi braced himself nonetheless. If Jonathan protested and Roger ignored the denial, Malachi would step in.

Meanwhile, he would watch. His own arousal grew by the moment, and he touched himself again through his trousers. He had no wish to watch someone taken against their will, but if Jonathan was willing, Malachi would enjoy the show. It would give him fuel for his own release.

"Will you let me?" Roger fumbled at the fastenings on Jonathan's trousers. Jonathan neither stopped nor aided him. "Will you, Jonathan? You promised."

"It will hurt." Jonathan sounded young then, and Malachi cringed.

Roger finally succeeded in his quest. He pushed Jonathan's trousers down and stroked the long prick that was revealed. "Does this hurt, Jonny?" Jonathan moaned, and Roger smiled. "I didn't think so. You like this, don't you?"

"It's nice," Jonathan murmured so softly Malachi wouldn't have heard him if not for shifter hearing, which was stronger than that of a human.

Malachi relaxed. Uncertainty, not refusal. That stimulated him, and he unfastened his own trousers so he could touch his bare prick. The men before him didn't speak again. The only sounds on the air were soft sighs and moans from Jonathan, whose eyes drifted closed. The expression on his face was pure pleasure as Roger manipulated his shaft. Roger bore a triumphant grin, which grated on Malachi somewhat. Roger knew he was succeeding in his seduction of the younger man and was proud of himself for it.

Perhaps before the encounter ended, Malachi would teach the dark-haired man some humility.

He let go of himself as Jonathan's soft sounds gave way to louder moans punctuated by sharp gasps. The man's climax was near, and Malachi leaned forward to see the lithe body tense, then buck as white fluid erupted from his cock. Malachi's mouth watered at the odor, which blended with the smell of the hooch and fed the fire inside him.

He needed release. Desperately.

"Wasn't that nice?" Roger asked in a low, persuasive tone. "You liked it, Jonny. Can't say you didn't."

"I liked it." Jonathan breathed deeply. "The rest of it, though… Can't I just do the same thing for you? Rub you like you just did me?"

"That isn't what you offered." Roger frowned. "Don't back out on me now, Jonny. If you back out on me, it's no hard thing to think you might back out on the bosses, and I'd hate to have to tell them you did that."

"You wouldn't." Jonathan's eyes widened. "They'd kill me!"

For a moment, Roger just looked with narrowed eyes at the younger man. Malachi growled again, his wolf to the fore and wanting to protect Jonathan for no reason he could discern. He readied himself to leap from the bushes if the confrontation took a bad turn. The blond didn't deserve this treatment, regardless of whom he'd become involved with.

Then Roger relaxed, and so did Malachi. "No," he said. "I won't. I take care of you, Jonny, don't I? I told you I won't let anything happen to you."

"You just said you'll tell them I'd back out on our deal." Jonathan stood a little straighter. In his mind, Malachi cheered him on. He should stand up to his friend, not just meekly take whatever was dealt. "Don't threaten me into letting you fuck me, Roger. That's no better than rape, and you told me you wouldn't let that happen either."

Roger didn't seem fazed by the accusation. "I'll keep my promises as long as you keep yours. We're short on time, Jonny. Now, or our deal is off. You liked what I just did for you, didn't you? I can do that again while I fuck you. It will make it much better. All you have to do is relax." He dropped his trousers, revealing a cock smaller than Jonathan's but still quite appealing. Malachi's hand stole to his own prick again without his realizing, and he rubbed himself while imagining that he had one hand on Roger and the other on Jonathan.

Jonathan's eyes widened again and he licked his lips. "That will fit in me?"

Roger's laughter echoed off the water. "Oh, it'll fit, Jonny. It'll fit nice. Just get on your knees and wet me up, and everything will be fine."

"You mean…?" Jonathan licked his lips again. Malachi had no doubt he knew exactly what Roger meant. And those lips looked so soft and perfect that Malachi was jealous that the rougher man would experience them.

Maybe later.

"Do it if you want me to take you easy," Roger said. "Otherwise it'll be dry, and believe me, that wouldn't be near as pleasant."

With no further argument, Jonathan dropped to his knees in the sand in front of Roger. The taller man stepped forward and brushed his prick against the blond's lips. Jonathan took the hint with only the slightest hesitation and allowed Roger to enter his mouth.

Malachi leaned forward, stroking himself more vigorously as the young man sucked the other, then released Roger's prick only to run his tongue up and down its length. The sight was the most erotic thing Malachi had seen, and he desperately wished that mouth was on him instead.

After only a few moments, Roger gasped, “Enough! I won’t spend in your mouth. That isn’t where it belongs.” The corners of his mouth quirked. “Not this time, at least.”

Jonathan rocked back on his heels and looked up at the other man. “Did I do it good?”

“Good enough. I was so close I almost didn’t stop you in time.” Roger extended his hand to help Jonathan to his feet. Malachi couldn’t help noticing how hard both men were, and his own cock became even harder in response to the sight. “Bend over that rock there. Looks to be the right height for our use.”

Jonathan didn’t hesitate at all this time to follow Roger’s order. He braced his arms on the rock, bending at the waist so his ass stuck out toward Roger. And toward Malachi, who found the rear view of the man just as attractive as the front.

Roger spat on his hand a couple of times and used the spittle to slick his fingers, then worked one wet finger into Jonathan’s hole. Jonathan shivered and let out a low moan. “Relax,” Roger said soothingly. “The more you relax, the better it will feel.”

Jonathan took an audible breath. Roger pulled his finger out and then inserted it again along with a second one. “See? It’s nice.”

“Y—yes,” Jonathan murmured. “It is.”

“My prick will be nice too.”

Oh, it would be. Malachi could stand no more. Clearly Jonathan had no objection to the events now unfolding, and Malachi wanted a closer look at the men’s sport. More, he wanted to fuck one of them. Either, at this point. Perhaps both, one after the other.

Slowly he crept forward, mindful of twigs and undergrowth that might crackle and herald his approach. The cool air on his shaft did nothing to soften it; if anything, the breeze brushing over it heightened his arousal. He gripped himself, stroking gently as he moved forward. Roger would take Jonathan. He could take Roger. That would be as near as possible to fucking them both at the same time, and the roaring hunger within him approved of the idea.

No. He stopped. He could not take Roger. Not without revealing his presence. Not without being asked.

Taking shallow breaths so they wouldn't hear, he stood back and watched Roger slowly work his prick into Jonathan's tight hole. The younger man tensed and whimpered, and Roger murmured soothing words. Despite his threats, it seemed he cared enough about his friend to try not to hurt him.

"There. It's in." Roger reached around to Jonathan's cock. "I'm going to fuck you now. Relax, Jonny. It only hurts until you relax. Then you'll like it. You'll see.

"Okay." Jonathan tensed again but relaxed just a bit when Roger's hand closed around his shaft.

Roger began slowly thrusting in and out of the blond's perfect ass. The sight was so beautiful Malachi nearly spent on the spot. His cock and balls ached for release. Taking himself in hand, he stroked his shaft in time with Roger's thrusts.

"I know you're there," Roger said.

Startled, Malachi stepped back.

"Wh—who's there?" Jonathan's voice cracked.

"It's all right." Pausing his movements, Roger peered over his shoulder. "You like what you see, mister? You can join."

"I'm sorry." His face heated, Malachi took another step backward. "I didn't mean…"

"Of course you did." Leering, Roger patted his own ass. "It's open. Jonny, you don't mind, do you? I'm fucking you, but I'd like a cock in my ass as well. And here's one hard and ready."

"I don't…" Jonathan moaned as Roger pulled back and pushed into him again. "Whatever you want, Roger."

An almost coquettish look in his eyes, Roger licked his lips. "Come on, then."

That look. That ass. The smell of spend and hooch and sea. Malachi gave over to the wolf and its lust. With a long stride, he closed the distance between himself and the other men. "Turn back to him. Fuck him."

"As you say." With another flick of his tongue on his lips, Roger turned and began slowly fucking Jonathan again. "Oh, Jonny, this is so good."

"Yes." Jonathan hissed the word.

Wrestling to hold onto his human mind and form, Malachi quickly spat on his hand and worked it along the length of his prick, then spat again onto his finger and touched the edge of Roger's hole.

"That's it," Roger murmured. "Take me."

Malachi pushed on the other man's shoulders. "Bend."

The word sounded more like a growl, but Roger seemed unfazed as he obeyed Malachi's command. Malachi smiled to himself. He didn't know how accustomed Roger was to taking a prick in his ass, but he met little resistance as he added a finger to the first and worked to stretch the small hole.

Roger stilled, and Malachi removed his hand. "Keep fucking him. His pleasure is your job right now."

"Have to stop to let you in." Gasps punctuated Roger's words.

"Very well. And then you'll give him his pleasure while I take mine."

"Yes."

Malachi positioned his prick at Roger's now stretched opening. He knew nothing about fucking an ass but having watched Roger take Jonathan, he understood that slowness was necessary. He eased forward, meeting more resistance but not enough to stop him.

As he pressed into Roger, both of the other men gasped. And then he was inside, balls-deep and ready to fuck.

He didn't even try to hold back. The human side of him didn't want to hurt the man, but the wolf side just wanted to move, to thrust, to find release. Pain was pleasure, and he sensed Roger was no stranger to either.

His thrusts pushed Roger into Jonathan, and the three moved by Malachi's rhythm. Roger gibbered and moaned. Jonathan let out small sounds that fueled Malachi's excitement. Malachi made no sound at all. He closed his eyes, savoring the tight friction. He gripped Roger's hips tightly and Roger squeaked. Not wishing to cause too much pain, Malachi loosened his hands slightly.

It had been too long since he'd felt anyone's touch but his own, and his climax built rapidly, fueled by his strokes earlier as much as by what he was doing now. Roger tensed and moaned, "It's coming. Oh, fuck."

"What?" Jonathan gasped. "Roger, don't—Please. Let me..."

The men's words barely reached Malachi's brain, but they were enough. He grunted loudly as sensation wiped away every thought. He retained barely enough control to hold his human mind and form.

The exquisite friction and tightness on his shaft brought his climax roaring down on him and he didn't even try to hold it at bay. The only thing in his mind other than pleasure was the wish that he'd indulged his attraction to men sooner. Heaven knew he'd had ample opportunity while at university, but he had always denied himself. He'd been with women, but that had never brought him the intense hunger and satiation that warred with each other now.

Roger groaned loudly, and Malachi gasped as pleasure burst into ecstasy so intense he thought he would faint. He exploded; he bucked; he roared his pleasure into the breeze. Through it all he remained aware of the wonderful friction of Roger's ass on his shaft and of the fact that Jonathan was likely having the same effect on Roger.

This was his first fuck with a man. He prayed it wouldn't be his last.

He opened his eyes as the climax faded. Roger bucked and stuttered against him, moaning through orgasm, and Malachi smiled. The man trembled and shook, and still Malachi remained inside him, though his own cock had begun to soften. He refused to leave that tight warmth until he had no other choice.

"P—please." Gradually Roger's trembling slowed. "Stop now."

"Did he spend?" Malachi leaned close so Roger would feel his breath. "He gave you what you wanted. Give him what he earned."

"I—please. Let me go now."

"Not yet." Malachi was determined. He'd had his pleasure, and Roger had had his. Jonathan had more than earned the same.

"It's all right," Jonathan murmured.

"No." Malachi withdrew abruptly from Roger, who gasped again. "If you won't stroke him, perhaps you'd prefer sucking him. Don't you dare stop until he's spent."

Roger glanced at Malachi. In the man's eyes, something kindled that told Malachi he enjoyed being ordered about. Malachi stored that information in case it was needed later and folded his arms. "Do it."

Roger pulled out of Jonathan. Jonathan whimpered and leaned forward on the rock. "Shit. Hurts."

"It'll hurt for a bit." Roger dropped to his knees. "I'll make you feel better. Turn around."

Jonathan moved slowly, wincing, until he faced Roger. Roger immediately engulfed Jonathan's prick with his mouth. Moaning, Jonathan dropped his head back and closed his eyes. Only seconds passed before he cried out and bucked against Roger. Tears streaked his cheek, something Malachi understood. Pleasure, pain, the first time—all overwhelming. Watching, he felt himself harden again and this time willed the arousal away. He had had what he needed for the moment. He adjusted his trousers and fastened them again. Now that he'd given way to the base desires within him, the alcohol's effect waned.

He should have expected it. Werewolves healed quickly, and it was logical that that would apply to drunkenness as well as injury.

Roger stood quickly and wiped his mouth with his hand. He

looked down at his softened cock and disgust fleeted across his expression. "I need to wash."

"There's a whole ocean right beside you." Malachi brushed past him to put his arm around Jonathan. "You're all right."

"It hurts." Jonathan looked into Malachi's eyes with his own startling deep blue ones. "I didn't know how much it would hurt."

"I didn't hurt you," Roger snapped. "Stop sniveling. We have to leave."

Without turning, Malachi reached back and grabbed Roger's arm. Roger yelped. "Shut the fuck up," Malachi snarled. "You don't get to tell him if he's hurt. You want to wash up, there's water beside you. He's coming with me."

"Where?" Jonathan shook. "He's right. We have to leave."

"You can take a few moments. My cabin's just up there." Malachi let go of Roger and nodded up the hill. "Salt water will sting too much. You can wash at my cabin."

"You think the water won't sting me?" Roger said.

Now Malachi whirled around. The other man shrank back. "I do not give a fuck if it stings you," Malachi said, enunciating each word. The man before him was nothing short of infuriating. He wanted to speak to the younger man alone, and that meant leaving Roger behind to take care of himself. "He'll be back shortly. You do not follow us. Do you understand?"

"Yes." Roger stared at the ground, the belligerence leaving him. In its place Malachi detected something like shame. "I didn't hurt him. I wouldn't."

"You did, but perhaps not intentionally." Malachi regarded the dark-haired man. Now that he had a good look, Roger appeared younger than he had initially. Older than Jonathan, and hard-used by Malachi's guess, but likely still in his twenties. He couldn't stay angry in the face of that knowledge. In a kinder tone, he said, "I won't hurt you, either. Just wait here."

Roger glanced up, and Malachi thought he saw gratitude in the other man's eyes. "Do you have a towel, at least? It'll be miserable if I can't dry off."

"I'll bring you one." Malachi narrowed his eyes. He felt a pang of guilt for frightening the man, but fear seemed to be a language Roger understood well and would obey. "Stay here. Clean up if you want, or don't." He took Jonathan's arm gently. "Come with me. I promise, you'll be safe."

Jonathan gulped, pulled up his trousers, and allowed Malachi to lead him up the hill. They moved slowly, and Jonathan let out several tiny sounds of pain as he walked. Malachi's anger rose, though he believed now that Roger hadn't intended pain. A woman's first fuck hurt; why wouldn't a man's first time being penetrated? Which reinforced, as indicated by Roger's behavior, that it hadn't been Roger's first time taking a cock. Roger had shown no sign of pain.

Neither spoke until they reached the cottage. "We thought no one would be here," Jonathan said as they stepped onto the platform in front of the door. "It's summer cottages, isn't it? That's what they said."

"Most of these places are vacant this time of year." Wondering who "they" were, Malachi guided Jonathan through the door into the cottage's kitchen with its running water. His father, a plumber, had installed sinks in both the kitchen and bathroom, as well as a flush toilet. He had planned to someday add a means of heating the running water, but hadn't done so before his death.

The more spacious kitchen would be the easiest place to wash up, along with giving Jonathan fewer steps to walk. Malachi turned on the faucet. "I live here all year. You and your friend were on my beach."

"We didn't know. They said no one would be here." He leaned against the counter beside the sink and winced again. "Does it always hurt like this?"

"I don't know. I suspect not, or people wouldn't keep doing it. Wait here." Malachi went into the room where he kept the linens and supplies his parents had left and found a few clean cloths. He wanted to wash himself as well, not to mention changing his clothing afterward.

When he returned to the kitchen, Jonathan's face was pale. "I think I'm bleeding."

"You might be a bit. Mostly you're feeling something else trickling. Here." He ran water onto a cloth, wishing he had some way to warm it. Ordinarily he heated water on the stove for washing up, but that would take time, and it sounded like Jonathan and Roger had no time. "Can you clean yourself?"

"I'm nineteen. I should think so." Anger flashed in Jonathan's eyes as he snatched the cloth from Malachi. Malachi hid a smile. Anger was always a good way to counter pain and fear. Jonathan started to push down his trousers, then looked up again. "Do you have to watch?"

"No." *But I'd like to.* Choosing to keep the comment to himself, he turned away and wet another cloth.

"Running water?" Jonathan said.

"It's 1930. People have running water." Malachi didn't understand the younger man's surprise, though he knew complete indoor plumbing was still rare in some of the cottages.

"I suppose." Jonathan said nothing more.

Malachi carefully cleaned his prick before going to his room for a clean pair of trousers. "I have to go," Jonathan called from the kitchen.

"Wait." Malachi dressed quickly and went back to the other man, who had already put his clothing back in order. "Why are you and Roger here?"

"How do you know our names?" The younger man's voice rose.

"I heard you talking. I'm Malachi."

Jonathan opened his mouth and closed it again. "Saying 'nice to meet you' seems odd."

"I expect so. Why are you here? You have hooch. What are you doing with it?"

"We don't—" Jonathan broke off, evidently realizing it would be futile to deny it. "We were hired. Part of a chain from another province. I don't know which. We picked it up in Peggy's Cove."

"You rowed here from Peggy's Cove?" It was a hell of a distance for a small boat like that.

"Didn't have any other way to get here. We stopped every so often to rest. This time, we just stopped off for—Well, you saw what we stopped for." His face reddened. "Roger's been good to me. I know it didn't seem it, but he saved me from being killed in Halifax. He's been looking out for me for two years. I needed money, needed work, and he said he'd cut me in on this deal if I—he's wanted me since we met. He told me he did but that he'd wait for me. I didn't understand at first. After a while, I knew what he wanted, and I said I would if he let me work with him this time."

Malachi carefully composed his expression. He couldn't imagine needing anything so badly as to trade his body for it, but in this time of Depression, people were desperate.

Apparently he wasn't careful enough. "I know how it sounds," Jonathan said. "You don't understand, and I don't have time to tell you the story. I needed the money, and Roger knew a way to get it. And…" He trailed off and looked at the floor. "I didn't mind the idea. I like men. I've known that for years. That's why I was on the street when Roger found me. My father forced me out of the house when he found out."

"I'm sorry." Malachi took the cloth from him and dropped it into the sink. It and the one he had used would need to be washed thoroughly. "I'd better take you back to Roger if you're sure you want to go."

"I haven't got a choice. They'll be waiting for us in Lunenburg. It's starting to get dark, and they said if we ain't there by full dark, they'll kill us." He said it in such a matter-of-fact tone that it took a second for the full meaning to dawn on Malachi. "It's going to take time to row around to the meeting place."

"Then let's go." Despite the urgency of the situation, Malachi paused. His heart ached to realize that this man had so little care for himself that the thought of being killed didn't matter. "If you need—you and Roger—you can come back here."

"They'd find us."

"I'd fight them." He blurted the words before thinking. "Trust me, anyone who came here trying to hurt you would find more than they bargain for. Let's go."

Now he moved quickly, giving Jonathan no time for the questions he doubtless had. He shouldn't have made such a promise, but the young man touched his heart, awakening a tenderness Malachi hadn't known was within him. He wanted Jonathan to stay. He wanted to take care of him. Even with his fiancée Malachi hadn't known such gentleness, and he couldn't just allow Jonathan to leave without offering some kind of help or hope.

He was out the door when Jonathan said, "I can't walk that fast."

"Sorry." Malachi stopped and waited while the other man slowly walked to him. "The pain should ease."

"Hope so. Maybe I can drink more of the hooch Roger opened. That'll cure anything." He gave Malachi a crooked smile. "Gives people ideas, too."

"So I noticed." Malachi refused to be embarrassed by his behavior, though it wasn't easy not to be. In a way, he'd done worse than Roger. Though he'd had consent for the fuck, neither man had agreed to his initial viewing of them. He'd peeped on them without their knowledge.

He led Jonathan back to the beach, where Roger was pacing back and forth beside the rowboat. Relief lit his face when he saw Jonathan and Malachi. "Thought you ditched me."

"I can't," Jonathan said. "I need to get paid." He turned and smiled again at Malachi. "Thank you."

"Come back if you need a place to hide." Malachi looked at Roger, including him in the invitation. He didn't think much of the dark-haired man, but Jonathan apparently did. And he had saved Jonathan, if the story was true. That was enough reason for Malachi to help him.

"Why would you want to offer that?" Roger asked, eyes narrowed.

"You're in a dangerous business." Malachi didn't know much about bootlegging, but even he had heard the stories of murders and maimings connected with the rumrunners. "Jonathan's afraid of your employers. You may be perfectly fine, but just in case, you can come back if there's need."

"Thank you," Jonathan said again. He elbowed Roger. "Let's get the crate back together. You said we have to make it look like it hasn't been opened."

"Right." Roger hunted around until he found a large stone. "Hold the lid in place."

Jonathan did, and Roger used the rock to hammer the lid back onto the crate. Malachi stepped back into the bushes as the men loaded the crate into the boat. He crouched as he had before, watching them. Though wondering at himself for the liberty he had taken with them, he wanted more. And he didn't want to say goodbye.

CHAPTER TWO

MALACHI waited up that night, reading by the light of an oil lamp while listening for footsteps outside the cottage. While he hoped Jonathan and Roger wouldn't need a place to hide, he also wished they would return. His invitation had been meant as an offer of safety, but also of more. He doubted Jonathan had heard it as such. He suspected Roger might have. The man was savvier than he acted. Malachi wondered how much time he had spent on the streets.

As time ticked past, he decided the men must have moved on after delivering their cargo. Disappointed, he shut off the lamp and went to bed.

He slept poorly that night. Regrets and thoughts of the evening's encounter kept him awake. At dawn, he gave up and returned to the cottage's living room with its large picture window overlooking the beach and bay.

A small boat moved through the water, aiming at the beach. Only one man occupied it. Malachi's vision wasn't quite as strong as his hearing or sense of smell, but it was good enough for him to recognize the rower as Roger.

Alone. Something must have happened to Jonathan.

Malachi didn't even pause for shoes. In only the trousers he'd pulled on upon rising from bed, he ran to the shore.

Roger paddled up to the beach, pushing against the bottom

of the bay with his oar. His eyes were wide, frantic, and he kept trying to move the boat even when it struck bottom. Malachi stepped into the water and pulled the boat up onto the sand. "Where is he? Where's Jonathan?"

"They—He—" Roger shook his head, swallowed hard, and tried again. "We drank one of the jugs. You saw, right? I made Jonathan drink it so he'd stop being so nervous."

"I saw." Malachi's lip curled at the reminder of the coercion Roger had used on his partner. And the effect the fumes had had upon him.

"We put the crate back together. We thought they wouldn't find out until we were out of there." He hung his head. "They found out. They said Jonathan had to stay with them until I made good on the deal. I have to get five jugs to replace the one, and I only have until tomorrow night to do it."

"Jonathan said you don't know where the hooch came from." Malachi extended his hand to the other man, who looked at it as if unsure what it was. "Get out of the boat and come to my cottage. We'll talk there in case they sent someone after you."

"Shit. I didn't think of that. Of course they want to make sure I don't bolt." He ran his hand through his greasy hair and stepped out of the boat, ignoring Malachi's attempted assistance. "I have to follow through. They'll kill him if I don't. I promised him he'd be safe. I can't break that promise."

"Come to my cottage," Malachi said again. "You're cold. Likely hungry, and certainly unsteady. Come warm up and eat. Coffee, maybe."

"How the fuck can I think about food and coffee!" Roger screamed the words into Malachi's face. "They have Jonathan!" Tears filled his eyes. "I promised him. I promised, and they have him, and I don't know how to save him!"

"Come with me." Malachi struggled to keep his patience. He, too, wanted to rush off and immediately rescue Jonathan. But his head ached and his thoughts were fuzzy. Although he'd shaken the immediate influence of the alcohol, apparently some effect, compounded by lack of sleep, had lingered. One hungover werewolf and a panicked young human wouldn't be able to do much except likely get themselves injured or killed.

Malachi shook his head to clear his mind. He could only hope that his tendency toward rapid healing would counter the remaining effects of his indulgence more quickly than a human would recover. Meanwhile, coffee and food would be the best thing for both of them.

"I'll carry you if I have to." He dropped his voice to a menacing level, hoping Roger would be motivated to follow his order. "It would be easier if you walked. If I carry you, I can't promise your head won't run into a few trees between here and my cottage."

"Fuck you." Roger's eyes were wild. If he'd been a shifter, he would have been on the verge of turning wolf.

"That would be one way to keep you still, wouldn't it? I got the feeling you don't mind being held down."

Roger roared and lunged at Malachi. Malachi easily stepped aside. When Roger made another attempt, Malachi grabbed him around the waist and lifted him from the ground as if he weighed nothing. Roger struggled, kicking Malachi's legs and pummeling his arms with fists that had little more effect than a mosquito.

"Stop," Malachi hissed. "I want him back safely. If we rush in, we might be caught too. And killed. Then where will Jonathan be?"

Roger's struggles slowed and he sobbed. "I tried to stop them."

"It isn't your fault." *Then whose is it?* This man had brought Jonathan into bootlegging. He'd brought him into danger. What had he expected from those who made their living smuggling hooch into the United States, a tea party? The men who ran the rumrunners could be dangerous, though the crews of the ships themselves were just local boys trying to support their families. If Roger had run up against the bosses, he was lucky he'd been allowed to leave.

He was lucky Jonathan hadn't been killed on the spot.

"If I put you down, will you come with me to my cottage?"

Malachi spoke more calmly, hoping that would in turn calm Roger.

Roger didn't respond for a moment. Malachi tightened his hold in case the man tried to flee. Finally, Roger nodded. "Yes. I'll go if you promise we won't wait long."

"I promise. You're half-starved. Food and drink while you tell me exactly what happened and where, and then we'll go find him." He doubted returning to Lunenburg in broad daylight would be wise. If the rumrunners saw Roger, they would know he wasn't completing their errand and might kill him and Jonathan anyway. But the sun was just rising, which meant they had little chance of reaching Lunenburg before daylight, and Malachi was damned if he would wait until nightfall.

"I'll go," Roger said again.

Malachi set the man on the sand. Roger stumbled on his first step, then caught himself.

"Stay beside me," Malachi said. He didn't trust the man not to run if he walked behind Malachi, and if he walked in front, Malachi would have to direct him the entire way. He doubted anyone was nearby, and if they were they had already heard Roger's outburst, but he still felt it best to be as quiet as possible.

The path was barely wide enough for two men to walk together. Malachi pushed through brush and branches, ignoring the scratches he received. They would heal.

Roger's eyes widened when he saw the cottage. "Hell, this is bigger than my family's house. People have places like this just for a few months a year? No wonder some of us starve."

Malachi chose not to answer. He'd heard enough diatribes against the wealth of families like his own. It wasn't their fault if others lived in poverty. This was a poor time to debate with Roger, as agitated as the man already was, so Malachi merely led him to the door and inside.

The sight of the cottage's interior did little to change Roger's reaction. "All this just for a summer place? My family would live a year off selling this stuff."

"I live here year-round." Malachi turned on the stove burner under the kettle he kept filled with water for hot drinks or, in a pinch, cleaning. "Feel free to look around. Don't get any ideas about stealing anything. After Jonathan's safe, if you and he still need money, I'll give you some items to sell." He had no attachment to most of his belongings. Much of the cottage's contents had been purchased by his parents when the cottage was built, less than two decades earlier. Only a few things had any sentimental value for him. He could easily spare some property if it meant getting Roger and Jonathan out of the bootlegging business.

"I'm not a thief," Roger said indignantly. He paused. "Except food. Been known to steal that a few times when it was either steal or starve."

"I'd say you made the better choice." Malachi didn't apologize for his assumption. Regardless of whether Roger had stolen in the past, the man was a criminal, engaged in illegal activity. If he was desperate enough to transport hooch, he might be desperate enough to slip a few knickknacks into his pocket to make some quick cash.

Roger wandered around the cottage's living room and three bedrooms while Malachi took out a pan and several eggs to cook for their breakfast. He wondered when Roger had eaten last and decided he didn't want to know.

After a few minutes, Roger entered the kitchen and leaned against the sink. "You live here alone?"

"My parents left me the cottage when they passed on. I have no one to share it with." That made him sound lonelier than he felt. He'd had ten years to accustom himself to being alone. He didn't mind it; he liked it. Or so he had convinced himself.

"Hell, Jonny and I'll share it with you. We wouldn't mind not being on the street for a while." He paused. "I tried to find work, you know. Honest work. Would have been better than what I'd been doing, and I didn't want Jonny into that. I didn't just decide to start bootlegging, but there wasn't nothing else. We have to eat."

"I'm not judging you." Malachi decided the eggs were cooked

enough and lifted the pan from the burner. He wanted to be sure they knew what they were doing before they went to Lunenburg, but he didn't want to delay too long. He closed his eyes for a moment, wishing he had some power to determine whether Jonathan was all right.

A faint sense tugged at his mind. Wishful thinking, perhaps, but he chose to believe it was an answer to his prayer. Jonathan hadn't been hurt—yet—and there would be time to rescue him. His captors wouldn't be likely to harm him during the time they'd given Roger to return with the additional jugs. They needed Jonathan to keep Roger in line.

Much like a criminal might use a man's wife or girlfriend. For the first time, it occurred to Malachi that perhaps Roger wasn't only trying to dominate the younger man. They'd been together for two years, Jonathan had said, and Roger had saved Jonathan's life.

Maybe Roger loved Jonathan. And maybe Jonathan returned those feelings.

Malachi's mind was too fuzzy to consider how he felt about the possibility of men being in love with each other. Sex was understandable. Sex felt good, regardless of whom one had it with. But love was something else entirely. Not that he knew much about that emotion.

"Plates are in the cupboard above you," he said. "Mugs, next to that. Get two of each, please."

Roger quickly followed the request. Malachi dished up the eggs and made two cups of coffee. He hoped Roger drank it black. That was how he himself took it, so there was little to put in it. Milk didn't get delivered out here, so he relied on tinned, and that had run out since he hadn't been willing to go for supplies lest the pack find him. Roger didn't complain when he picked up a cup, though.

"We'll eat at the table," Malachi said.

Roger followed him into the main room without a word. The side of the room nearest the kitchen had been designated the dining room, with a long table his parents had purchased with the intention of hosting guests. Malachi sat at the head of the table, where his father had always sat during his childhood, and motioned for Roger to take the chair beside him. Roger did so and began shoveling eggs into his mouth, barely pausing for breath.

"You were hungry." Malachi sipped his coffee. He didn't feel especially hungry himself. His stomach was a bit unsteady. But he had learned the hard way that as a werewolf, he needed more food than a human would, so he started slowly eating his eggs.

"Haven't eaten since yesterday," Roger said through a mouthful. He swallowed and added, "Or the day before. Can't remember, to be honest. The last thing was some bread we nicked off someone's windowsill near where we picked up the hooch."

Malachi wondered whether the bread's owner had been too trusting or had left the food there with the intention of it being taken by someone in need. Those who had enough—and even those who didn't—sometimes helped out those with less. Something he would do well to try himself.

"It isn't good to go so long without food," he said.

The look Roger gave him might have killed a weaker man. "You think we don't know that? It ain't like we can just waltz into a place and ask for caviar or whatever shit people like you eat. Sometimes we get food. Sometimes we don't. I take care of Jonathan before me if I can."

Malachi held up a hand. "I didn't mean to offend you. I know you do the best you can. Everyone does these days, it seems. I don't hear much about the rest of the world. I stay here except when I need provisions. Then I go into Lunenburg, or across to Mahone Bay if it's warm enough for a row, get what I need, and come back."

"Hermit." Roger stuffed enough eggs into his mouth to choke a man and swallowed without apparently chewing. "Thanks for the food. You got enough for Jonathan after we get him?"

"Not quite." He was running low on nearly everything. The packs hadn't approached him thus far. Perhaps making a supply run would be safe enough. The other wolves tended to avoid town, as he understood it; the only risk would be while traveling, and he and Roger could do that by sea. "I'll have to go to the shops, but that isn't a bad thing. That can be my excuse for being in Lunenburg. Most people there won't have seen you when you brought the hooch. I can say I hired you to help me carry things because I'm buying extra for the winter."

"Are we walking, or you got a car stashed around here?"

"No car." He hadn't seen the point in one when he left Herman's Island only once or twice a month, less in winter when snow made it more difficult to get up the dirt track that led to the main road. He could walk to town most of the year or go by boat. A car would be more extravagant than he could justify. "We would have walked, but I honestly do need to buy some things. We'll take my boat. It'll be longer till we get there, but the rumrunners are based on the waterfront, aren't they?"

Roger nodded with another mouthful of eggs. Malachi was glad he'd made so much. He'd feared some would go to waste, but there was clearly no danger of that.

Roger swallowed finally and said, "Used to be a boat builder shop. I guess it still is, except now they're building rumrunning boats. And the runners get their deliveries and leave for the States from there. Heading for Gloucester, mostly, since there's already connections between Gloucester and Lunenburg."

The not-always-friendly rivalries between Lunenburg fishermen and those from Gloucester, Massachusetts, were legend. Malachi wasn't surprised that Gloucester men worked with the Lunenburg rumrunners. Both groups were likely starving. There was no shortage of fish in the ocean, so fishermen might catch enough to feed their families, but in this time of no jobs and no money, the fishermen were probably not finding much market to sell what they caught. Smuggling alcohol meant money for both sides.

"So we'll tie up to the wharf nearest there and walk up to the shops," Malachi said. "Might not be a good idea to barge in to get Jonathan right off. In daylight, we'd be too easily caught."

An idea started to form in his mind. In daylight, they would be noticed. He had no question about that. He could move silently enough through the woods around the cottage, but daytime in town would mean people. The rumrunners would probably have folks guarding their shop, making sure no one stole their contraband from them. He suspected they slept in shifts, so he and Roger would never find a time when no one was guarding the shop and Jonathan. But at night, a wolf might move more easily through the streets. People tended to stay indoors after dark.

A wolf would seem no threat to the rumrunners. He might even be able to walk right into the shop.

Werewolves weren't allowed to reveal themselves to humans. That was one of the first lessons Malachi had learned upon recovering from his change. But he was already a lone wolf, what some might call a rogue, and the rules of the world he'd been forced into meant little. Revealing his true nature to Roger and Jonathan would sentence him to death, but he likely already faced that. He couldn't be killed twice.

"I might have a plan," he said. "I can't tell you just now. I need to see the place they're holding him first. And it'll need darkness to succeed anyway."

"We can't leave him there overnight!" Roger shoved his plate away with such force it slid off the other side of the table to shatter on the floor. "He's scared, damn it! You don't know what they might do to him. One of them kept talking about how pretty he is."

"Those men are mostly fishermen. Family men." Malachi hoped he sounded like he knew what he was talking about. "They might try to frighten him by saying such things, but it's unlikely they would take him."

"That's what you know." Roger stood, and his chair toppled over. "You don't know what criminals will do to shame anyone who goes against them. You don't know what they'll do to show they're in charge."

Malachi didn't know, but from Roger's reaction he could well imagine. He shuddered at the thought of such things being done to Jonathan—or to Roger, who, he judged, had experienced it first-hand.

He made the effort to speak calmly, lest Roger lose his temper to the point of destroying the cottage. "I haven't seen it for myself, no. But most of these men, especially those who captain the boats, aren't criminals, are they? They're fishermen, working men. They aren't in this to break the law. They're in it to keep food on their tables until things turn around. If they're the ones minding the shop, they won't hurt Jonathan. They might say they will, especially if they're told to say it, but they won't do it."

"You'd best hope you're right." Roger narrowed his eyes. "If anything happens to him because we didn't get there in time, it's on your head."

"All right." They would be in time. He was certain of it. "They're expecting you to bring more hooch. They're holding him to give you a reason to come back. Until your time's up, I don't think they'd hurt him, because then they wouldn't have anything to hold over you."

Roger's glare deepened for a moment, then he nodded. "Okay. You could be right. I don't want to wait any longer, though."

"Clean up after yourself first." Malachi nodded toward the broken plate and bits of egg on the floor behind the table.

Roger looked sheepish. "Sorry about that. Lost my temper."

"I understand. Just clean it and we'll forget about it. The broom is beside the ice box."

While Roger swept up, Malachi finished his food and coffee. He would need the fortification, and the caffeine, to get through the rest of the day.

He left his dish and the two cups in the sink. Washing up wasn't important enough to delay the trip into town any longer. Roger threw the pieces of plate and egg into the trash bin and put the broom and dustpan back where he'd found them. "I'm sorry," he said again.

Malachi had the sense that the words didn't come easily for

him. “It’s just a plate,” he said. “I appreciate you sweeping it up. Wouldn’t want anyone cutting their feet. Let’s go. My boat’s under the verandah. You’ll have to help me carry it down to the water.”

“Why don’t we take mine? It’s already there.”

“They might know yours.” Malachi found his shoes in a corner of the main room and put them on. “If anyone sees mine, they’ll just figure it’s the hermit again.”

“Is that really how they think of you?”

Malachi nodded. “They see me in town once in a while and never otherwise. Most assume that I live somewhere away from town. Most know me, since I grew up there. They think something happened to me at university to change me, and they know I lost my parents last year, so they’re kind and don’t ask any questions.” The people of Lunenburg didn’t know how right they were. They just didn’t know what change had occurred. They assumed insanity of some sort. Given the nature of werewolves, “lunacy” would have been more accurate.

“Will they ask about me?” Roger sounded more than a little concerned about the possibility.

“As I said, if they do, I’ll say you came around looking for work and I hired you to help me lay in provisions for the winter. It’s September. That will be explanation enough, since even with help, it will take more than one trip to bring home enough for a few months.”

“I can’t even imagine having enough money to buy that much food.” Roger shook his head. “Do you even know how lucky you are?”

“I’m beginning to realize.” Hearing the raw envy in Roger’s tone made Malachi uncomfortable. “Let’s go.”

They pulled the rowboat out from the storage space beneath the cottage’s verandah. Malachi’s father had built the place on a slope, which left plenty of room below to keep things that wouldn’t fit inside the cottage, while avoiding the need for a separate shed or boat house. He gave the bottom of the boat a cursory inspection to ensure that he and Roger wouldn’t sink on their way to town, and then they carried the boat down to the beach.

"Lot of trouble to go to just to get to town." Roger was out of breath by the time they reached the water. "Be easier if you had a car."

"The roads aren't the best," Malachi replied. "This suits me fine. We should get your boat higher up, maybe into the bushes. Tide will take it otherwise, and if anyone comes looking for you, we wouldn't want them spotting it."

"Yeah." Roger frowned. "I didn't think of that. They might already have seen it."

"If they did, they did. We should still move it. The tide's coming in." Already it was lapping at the bow of Roger's little boat, whereas when Roger had arrived the water had only reached the boat's midpoint.

They pulled the boat up into the bushes where Malachi had hidden the previous day and climbed into Malachi's boat. Looking at the sun, he estimated the time to be around seven thirty. By the time they arrived in Lunenburg, most shops would be open. That was the only advantage to the trip taking so long.

He made Roger get into the boat and pushed it off into the water before climbing in himself. Cursing himself for not taking off his shoes, he took position in the boat's stern and started rowing.

"I can help," Roger said.

"Rest," Malachi replied. "Sleep if you want. I can manage." He doubted the man was nearly as strong as he was. Increased strength was another side effect of being a werewolf.

Roger sat on the bench in the boat's bow, facing Malachi. "Why are you so concerned?"

"You came to me for help," Malachi pointed out. "And I may be a hermit, but that doesn't mean I have no heart. How long have you been on your own?"

"On my own?" Roger sniffed. "I'm twenty-three years old. You make it sound like I'm a child."

To Malachi, the man seemed like a child. A tough one, streetwise and too knowing, but a child nonetheless regardless of his age. "Jonathan said you were on the street when he met you."

"That." An unreadable expression crossed Roger's face. "Left home when I was twelve. I had reasons. Don't want to get into them, if that's all right with you." His tone made it clear he didn't care whether it was all right.

"You don't have to tell me anything you'd prefer not to," Malachi assured him. "I don't mean to pry. You might have guessed I don't speak with others often. But if you're not going to sleep on the way to town, we might as well talk to pass the time."

Roger shrugged. "My father was a fisherman. Died on the water when I was eight. When I was eleven, my mother remarried. Another fisherman, one who did more drinking than fishing. He was free with his hands and expected me to be free with other things, if you catch my meaning."

Malachi caught it perfectly and swallowed hard against a roll of nausea. He wasn't naïve; he knew some men did horrible things to their families. But hearing Roger discuss it so matter-of-factly made his heart ache. "Did you tell your mother?"

"What could she do? He used his fists on her as much as me, and she said we needed him to keep a roof over our heads." He looked down at his hands. "I took it once. Not that he gave me much choice. Hurt like hell. He wasn't gentle. He didn't care. I think he liked hurting me that way. I'd just turned twelve then, thought maybe I could find work in the city, so I went."

"And did you find work?" Malachi braced himself for the answer he anticipated. He doubted a twelve-year-old boy on his own had found a job in a shop or on a ship.

"Of sorts." Roger's voice dropped. Even with his heightened hearing, Malachi had to strain to make out the words through the wind in his ears. "There were men who wanted the same thing as my stepfather. Some of them were gentler, and they paid. It kept me fed. Gave me shelter, sometimes. It wasn't what I wanted, but all in all it might have been worse. At least I lived."

Malachi's heart went out to this young man, who had lived by means no one should have had to. And he had done nothing better than the men who'd purchased Roger's body. "I apologize for what I did to you yesterday. I should have left you and Jonathan alone."

"What?" Roger looked at him, surprised. "No. I didn't mind that. I could have fought you off if I'd wanted. I—I'd done that kind of thing before. Some of the johns liked it, two of them and one of me. I didn't mind. I asked you, didn't I?"

"You did. But I shouldn't have been there to begin with." Malachi's stomach rolled again. He tried to blame it on his hangover, but that had already faded thanks to food, coffee, and rapid werewolf healing. The truth was, in his drunkenness he had victimized one who had been victimized too many times before. He sickened himself.

"Nor should we." Roger shrugged again. "Didn't mind it, I told you. Truth be told, I liked it. You were easy. Took your time. It was nice."

"I watched you with Jonathan," Malachi confessed. "I saw how you made it easier for him and did the same. I almost stopped you with Jonathan. At first, it seemed like you would take him against his will."

Roger's face reddened. "I shouldn't have bullied him, but he'd been waffling for days. I'd let him know right after I found him that I was interested, but I never pushed, not for two years. Not ever until yesterday. He came to me and said if I helped him get some money, he'd let me have him. I didn't want to. It felt like I'd be buying him. Like I'd be doing what the johns did to me. Hell, I tried talking him out of it! The fool said he needed the money and would rather give himself to me than a john. So I said okay, and then he spent days back and forth between yes and no. He was afraid, see. Not of me, but of wanting it. Of liking it."

"I understand." Given the reason Jonathan had stated for leaving home, of course he wouldn't want to be thought of as a man who enjoyed sex with men. Even though he clearly trusted Roger, he might even have feared losing his friend by giving himself to him.

"I asked him if he wanted to back out," Roger said. "Before we got here, I said we could change the deal. He said no, that he wanted to go on with it but might need persuading. So I persuaded." He looked up again, raw anguish in his expression. "You were alone with him yesterday. Did he say I forced him? He didn't want it?"

"No, no." Malachi felt the man's pain. He had to let Roger know that he hadn't hurt his friend. "Nearly the opposite. He said he hadn't expected to be so sore afterward, but that he'd agreed to it. Just like you said."

"I love him." Roger said it in the same matter-of-fact tone in which he'd discussed his stepfather's abuse, but the fear in his eyes told Malachi he expected revulsion at the least. "It's wrong, I know that. Been told enough times what should be done to faggots. But I love him, and I brought him into this so we'd have enough money to make things better for us both. Maybe go out west. I heard there might be work there."

"Might be." It was on the tip of Malachi's tongue to ask Roger to stay. Him and Jonathan both. Roger himself had pointed out how ridiculous it was for Malachi to live alone in the cottage, a place easily large enough for three. He could take care of them, and they would be company for him.

The urge was laughable. He tolerated people for the sake of staying fed and clothed; he couldn't create items out of thin air, after all. But living with not one but two men? He didn't know if he would be able to take that for a long period of time.

Not to mention the fact that once each month, he had no choice but to shift into wolf form and run through the woods. He had discovered that during most of the month, he could choose whether to be human or wolf, but the full moon took the choice out of his hands. It was all he could do to make sure he wasn't seen by the humans who summered on the island. He wouldn't be able to avoid Roger or Jonathan, and that meant they would learn what he was. At the very least, they would be afraid of him.

He couldn't provide a home for anyone but himself, no matter how much he wanted to.

"You okay?" Roger asked. "You got this odd look."

"Fine. Tired." Malachi forced a smile. "It sounds like you've taken good care of Jonathan since you met him."

"I didn't want him ending up like me." Roger slumped down and closed his eyes. "Think I will sleep, if that's all right. I'm tired of talking."

"I told you to sleep." Malachi wanted to continue the conversation, but Roger clearly had grown uncomfortable with it. If he wanted the man to trust him, he had to respect his feelings. He'd likely told Malachi more than anyone else, except perhaps Jonathan, and Malachi didn't want to cause any more strain. He wouldn't have said so, but he admired Roger both for surviving what he'd been through and for protecting Jonathan from a similar fate. The man might have been a petty criminal, but he had a heart and strength that awed Malachi.

CHAPTER THREE

MALACHI didn't know whether Roger truly slept or only pretended, but the other man kept his eyes closed for the rest of the trip. The repetitive motion of rowing and the movement of the waves beneath the boat lulled Malachi into a near trance for which he was thankful. He had no need to think, only to continue raising and lowering the oars. It was the nearest he ever came to peace.

By the sun's position, he estimated they arrived in Lunenburg somewhere between half past eight and nine o'clock, though he couldn't pinpoint it any more exactly than that. He tied the rowboat in an open space at one of the docks, conveniently beside a ladder, and nudged Roger. "We're here."

Roger blinked several times, yawned, and stretched. "Already?"

"You slept. It wasn't a short trip." Malachi nodded at the buildings along the waterfront, most painted red with green trim. "Which one is it?"

"There." Roger pointed to the building at the end of the line. Two low-slung boats were tied to the dock in front of it. "They're waiting to send out another shipment."

"Waiting for you," Malachi guessed.

Roger nodded. "They can't send a short crate, they said. They want to replace the missing jug. Don't know what they plan to do with the other four they told me to fetch. Probably drink it."

"I wouldn't be surprised." Malachi studied the building. He suspected men would be guarding the dock and boats, which meant approaching it from the water side would be foolhardy at best. The street side might be less closely watched by the rumrunners, so that would be the best way to enter. But Malachi saw several people strolling along the street, along with a sparse handful of cars. He and Roger couldn't go anywhere near the building at this point without being seen and likely questioned.

"We might have to leave him till after dark," he said. "If I say that's how it needs to be, I want your word that you'll go along with it."

"Are you fucking loony?" Roger's voice cracked. "Bad enough he's been alone in there this long, and now you want to leave him through the day?"

"Look." Malachi nodded toward the street, where a woman carrying a large covered basket was approaching the boat shop. From their vantage point, he couldn't see her at the front of the building, but he believed his assumption to be correct. She was bringing food to the men inside. And that likely included Jonathan. "They'll feed him, Roger. He may be safer in there than anywhere else at the moment. Yes, they'll be watching him, and they won't let him go until you return. If you don't bring back the hooch they demanded, you and Jonathan will be in danger. Until then, I think they'll treat him all right. The bosses, as you say, are dangerous men, but most of the men in there aren't the bosses. They're fishermen and they have no reason to be cruel to Jonathan."

He might be putting far too much faith in these working-class men. If one of their bosses offered them money to beat Jonathan or worse, there were at least one or two who'd take it because it would mean extra food for their families. On the other hand, these men had hearts and souls. They weren't thugs. Most, if not all, had lines they wouldn't cross.

Roger took a few deep breaths, visibly struggling to keep his temper. “You done this before?” he asked finally.

Malachi shook his head with a small smile. “No, I can’t say I’ve ever saved a small-time smuggler from a group of rumrunners. I just know this town. I grew up here. People here still attend to what their neighbors are doing. The men in there mostly have families and friends, and they will be protective. Didn’t you say they told you and Jonathan to come here after dark?”

“Yes.” Roger paused. “They didn’t want us to be seen. People would see you and me if we went there now.”

“Right.” Malachi had said that before. It apparently hadn’t sunk in previously. Roger was so determined to rescue his friend that he refused to hear any reasons against it.

They aren’t merely friends. Malachi found the idea less surprising than before. Roger loved Jonathan, and Jonathan likely returned the feeling. The fact that Roger was willing to risk himself to save Jonathan showed devotion Malachi hadn’t seen in some married couples, his own parents included. As did the fact that despite his desires, Roger had waited two years to have Jonathan sexually. Even then, if Roger’s story was to be believed, he had tried to talk Jonathan out of it.

Of course Roger wouldn’t want to wait until dark. He knew only that his friend—his *lover*—was in danger and was away from him. And since Roger had brought Jonathan into bootlegging, he almost certainly blamed himself for Jonathan’s capture.

“This isn’t your fault, you know,” he said.

Roger furrowed his brow. “What are you talking about?”

“The rumrunners keeping Jonathan. It isn’t your fault.”

“Fuck you,” Roger spat. “I’ve been doing this a while now. Told Jonathan I had a delivery job from outside the city down here to Lunenburg but wouldn’t tell him more. For a while, he didn’t ask too many questions. I gave him money and food. Even got us a room last month in a real rooming-house. I might not have been earning it legal, but I was earning, and I was trying to make our lives better with it.”

"I know you were," Malachi said gently. And again the comparison to married couples crossed his mind. Just as many a young husband took whatever work he could find to put a roof over the head of his wife, Roger had chosen to smuggle hooch to provide a home for Jonathan. Not only that. He'd tried to prevent Jonathan from finding out where the money came from.

"Then he got all jittery one day. Said he needed money bad and wanted to help me work." He closed his eyes and shuddered. "He borrowed from someone he shouldn't have. He didn't know any better. The fucking little fool borrowed five dollars to buy food and gifts for my fucking birthday."

"That's quite a sum." Malachi sensed that under Roger's anger and fear lay some happiness. Jonathan had cared enough to borrow money to provide him a celebration.

"Too much a sum when he borrowed from a criminal," Roger muttered. "He was given a week to pay it back, and of course he didn't have it. He didn't know that every day, they added another five to what he owed. He's into them for at least a hundred now. He owed near fifty when he confessed to me. I should have watched him better. He doesn't know how to live out there. I don't know how he made it before I found him. He's not stupid, just innocent."

"You thought he'd be safe with you," Malachi said, putting together the rest of the story. He did a quick mental calculation. He wasn't as wealthy as he'd once been, but he believed he could clear Jonathan's debt. And if the debtor showed reluctance about accepting the money, Malachi could exercise a bit of lupine persuasion. Sharp teeth in the mouth of a large wolf could be quite convincing.

Roger nodded. "We were getting twenty apiece for this job. I was going to give him my share and go with him to talk to the shark. We'd give them the forty and negotiate more time to get the rest. I thought I could keep him safe. I'm as much a fool as him."

"You've done more for him than anyone ever did for you." Malachi's anger rose as he remembered what Roger had said about his own life. No one had cared for him, and yet he'd found it in himself to protect someone he could easily have preyed on.

"I did for him what he needed done." Roger started to stand but quickly dropped back onto the bench when the boat rocked. "Are we just going to sit here?"

"No." Malachi held out his hand. The other man was clearly embarrassed by praise. Malachi hoped that wouldn't always be the case. Roger had a rough past, but there were things about him to admire as well.

Roger took his hand, and Malachi pulled the other man to his feet. Roger looked startled when the boat rocked again, and Malachi reassured him. "Just take hold of the ladder and climb up. You act like you've never been in a rowboat before."

"I act like this every time. I'm always afraid I'll fall over." He looked sheepish. "Never had much to do with boats before I started this job."

"You'll learn. Climb up so I can."

Roger quickly scaled the ladder to the dock's surface, and Malachi followed. None of the few passers-by seemed surprised by seeing two men on the dock. Malachi took that as a good sign. Some of them probably recognized him. Some just took it for granted that people came into town by boat as often as by other means when the weather allowed it.

"We're going to buy food," he said to Roger. "We'll bring it back to my cottage and come back later, after dark. I know you don't want to leave him, but right now, we'd have no chance of getting in and out of there without being stopped."

"There'll be more men in there at night," Roger argued. "That's when the bosses show up to make sure the shipments are right."

"There'll be fewer women and children around at night," Malachi said. "And less chance of us being seen outside the boat shop. We'll be harder to follow, too." And he would be able to shift into his wolf form more easily.

Naturally he didn't say that to Roger. A time might come when he would have to tell Roger and Jonathan everything, but this was not that time.

"You're older than me," Roger said. "Doesn't mean you know more."

"True. It does, however, mean that I'm in charge here, and you'd already agreed to waiting until nightfall to rescue Jonathan." He didn't know whether proclaiming himself in charge would anger Roger or make him more compliant. Nor did he particularly care which result he achieved. They were wasting time standing here, and with each second it became more likely they would attract attention.

The same thought may have occurred to Roger, because he let out a long breath and his anger visibly faded. "All right. You can be in charge if that pleases you." He chuckled, not pleasantly. "Does it please you? Maybe we ought to find out later, back at the cottage."

"Or not." Malachi found the suggestion distasteful, particularly in public. "I suggest we save that type of discussion for a more appropriate setting."

"You're a stiff one, ain't you." Roger laughed, likely at his double meaning. "Yeah, fine, in public, respectable people, and so on. Let's get the errand-running over with."

He walked swiftly to the street end of the dock and turned, looking back expectantly at Malachi. Malachi sighed. The other man was rough, no question. Even had Malachi not known Roger's history, his behavior spoke of one who had lived on the streets and had had no guidance in his life.

For whatever reason, that appealed to Malachi. The outrageousness of Roger's words was disturbing but also amusing. With Roger, no time could ever be dull. After so many years on his own, having convinced himself it was what he preferred, Malachi longed for someone else to share his time with and keep him occupied.

That discussion, too, would wait until they had rescued Jonathan. He wanted to present it to both men together, because although it might only have been the results of lust and loneliness, he wanted both of them to stay.

He walked up the dock and, without a word to Roger, up the

hilly street toward the shop where he typically made most of his purchases. A few people spoke to them. Malachi answered abruptly, as was his habit, and introduced Roger as he'd said he would. Roger played along, giving the name "Jericho" when asked and hanging his head as if ashamed to be so desperately out of work that he would carry groceries for the town's eccentric hermit.

They managed most of the trip without incident, until they, with the help of a borrowed handcart and the too-friendly young son of the grocer, toted Malachi's purchases back to the dock. When they reached the corner opposite the boat shop, Roger froze. "They're watching. He ain't one of the townsfolk. He's one of the big ones."

Malachi looked in the same direction. A stocky older man stood in front of the boat shop, arms folded, surveying the street. Instinctively, Malachi stepped in front of Roger. His mind raced frantically for a solution to the problem this posed. If Roger recognized the man, the man would almost certainly recognize Roger. He would see them when they approached the boat. There was no way to avoid it.

"I got to get the cart back," the grocer's son, a boy of ten or twelve, said. "Dad will want it for other customers."

"One moment." Malachi pulled a crumpled bill from his pocket and, without checking to see its amount, held it out to the boy. "That will pay for your father's trouble."

"Thanks!" The boy's surprised exclamation echoed off the building beside them.

The man in front of the boat shop turned to look. An anguished whimper from Roger forced Malachi to think more quickly. "Take some things out of the cart," he said. "Carry them in front of you. I'll guide you till we're out of his sight."

"He'll see me." Roger sounded terrified. "He'll tell them all I'm here instead of on my way to pick up the—what they said to get."

"No, he won't." Malachi grabbed a couple sacks from the cart and shoved them into Roger's arms. "Carry them high so your face can't be seen."

"Should I get the police?" The young boy looked around, an eager smile on his face. "Is there a bad guy after you? I saw this picture with bad guys."

"This is no picture," Malachi said. "And no, no one's after us. Tell you what, why don't you go let your father know we've been a bit delayed? I'll bring the cart back after we've unloaded it."

"I'm not supposed to let customers alone with it. Dad's afraid it'll walk off like the last one."

Malachi fumbled another bill out of his pocket and gave it to the boy. "I'll bring it right up. I'm sure your father could use your help right about now."

"Okay." The boy's face brightened and he ran back up the street.

With the child safely out of the way, Malachi took the handles of the cart. "Walk against the back of the cart," he told Roger. "Keep the sacks up high. You won't be able to see where you're going, but as long as you feel the cart against your legs, you'll be fine."

"I'm trusting you." Roger moved behind the cart. "I hope that doesn't make me foolish."

So do I. Malachi glanced at the boat shop. The man was looking in the opposite direction now. Perhaps he'd decided that the strangers with the handcart were nothing more than they appeared, men bringing provisions to a boat. He prayed there would be no further problems.

He pulled the cart and led Roger across the street and down the dock to the ladder. The tide had come in more while they'd shopped, and their boat sat closer to the dock's surface now, which would make it easier to load their purchases. "Get into the boat and I'll hand things to you," he told Roger. "Make sure you place them evenly. We don't want too much weight in one spot."

"I know how to load boats." Roger dropped the sacks back into the cart and scrambled down the ladder.

"Hey, could you use some help?" a voice called from the street.

Malachi's heart pounded. He looked down at Roger's wild eyes and knew the offer must have come from the man they'd seen. He looked toward the voice and sure enough, the man was approaching them.

"He—"

Malachi motioned for Roger to stay silent and turned to face the man. "No, thank you."

"This isn't the best place to tie up." The man didn't stop walking toward them. "You never know what might be happening here."

"Let us load our boat and we'll leave." Deliberately looking away from the man, Malachi picked up a sack and passed it down to Roger. Roger frantically shook his head. Heart racing, Malachi narrowed his eyes, wishing he had some way to direct Roger that the stranger wouldn't hear. As it was, he could only use movements and gestures to make Roger take the sack and lay it in the bottom of the boat.

"What do you have there?" The man was now beside Malachi. "Looks like quite a bit. Sure you couldn't use a hand?"

"I hired someone to give me a hand," Malachi said. Visions of a trussed-up Jonathan being thrown in the harbor flashed through his mind. He had to get this man away from him and Roger before Roger was recognized. "We can manage, thank you."

He straightened and positioned himself between the man and the ladder. To see Roger, the man would have to come closer to the edge of the dock. Malachi would do whatever proved necessary to keep that from happening. Up to and including tossing the man into the water. Even if the man could swim, the shock of entering the water would slow him down enough to allow Roger time to escape.

"It'll be faster with another pair of hands," the man said. "My boss doesn't really appreciate people using this dock."

"I apologize," Malachi said. "I've tied up here before. I didn't know it was private property."

"It's just in use." The man folded his arms and glowered. "I'd like to get you on your way."

"I'd like to avoid having too many hands on my supplies." Speaking nearly as quickly as he could think, Malachi went on, "I don't like having my belongings touched. Nothing personal. Just my preference."

"I think I've heard about you." The man's expression relaxed slightly. "You live off in a summer colony, right? Come into town once in a while for food and otherwise no one ever sees you?"

"That's right." For once, Malachi was thankful for small-town gossip. It was quite logical that he would be a topic of it. There wasn't much excitement in a town like Lunenburg, other than storms and boats returning late from fishing trips. Speculating about the odd man from one of the town's most prominent families would relieve a lot of boredom.

"So you hired a total stranger to help you?"

The man's skeptical tone put Malachi immediately on guard. "I have a soft spot for those who've lost work because of the Depression," he said. "He found his way to me by boat and begged for work. I felt that much initiative should be rewarded."

"I see." The man didn't look as though he believed Malachi for a moment. Malachi braced himself for more questions, hoping his brain would prove up to the task of answering. "I suppose I understand," the man said finally. "Good luck to you, then."

He glanced down at the boat, where Roger had fortunately bent down to hide his face under the guise of arranging the sacks Malachi had handed him. Shrugging, the man gave Malachi a slightly disgusted look and walked away.

Only then did Malachi realize the man had assumed he was homosexual and had taken Roger as a lover.

Which isn't far off the truth. Not at all off, if Malachi was honest with himself. He took a few deep breaths, trying to calm himself. The man was gone, which meant the danger of Roger being recognized was as well. But Malachi's instincts had been roused, and the wolf inside him seemed to pace and growl, needing release. He wouldn't feel completely calm and safe until he and Roger were out of town.

“That was too close,” Roger said.

“I’ll hand down the rest. Once everything’s in the boat, go.” Malachi picked up another sack and gave it to him. “I’ll make my own way back by land.”

“I don’t want to leave you behind,” Roger said. “Unless you’re going after Jonathan without me.”

“I’m waiting for dark for that, as I said.” Malachi mentally added loyalty to the surprising qualities Roger possessed. “I promised the boy I’d return the cart, and I won’t break that promise. I don’t think it would be safe for you to wait here for me.”

“I could wait around the other side.”

“I’d rather you just get these things back to the cottage. Anyway, the boat can’t carry both of us with all these supplies. Too much weight.” Malachi was becoming frustrated with the man’s arguments, though he recognized fear as one of the reasons behind them. Roger didn’t want to be alone on the water or at Malachi’s cottage.

But Malachi itched for a run, after all the stress the day had brought him, and he certainly wouldn’t be able to shift in a boat. He would be able to run that night, but he needed something sooner. Once outside town, he would be able to find a wooded area where he could shift without being seen, and he would be unlikely to encounter humans between there and home. He’d done it before.

He passed more down to Roger. “Do you trust me, Roger?”

“As much as anyone, I guess.”

Malachi wasn’t surprised that trust was something Roger gave reluctantly. “Then trust when I say you’ll be best off leaving as soon as the boat’s loaded, and that I will meet you at the cottage. You can row the boat back alone, can’t you?”

“Rowed myself there this morning, didn’t I?” Roger said indignantly.

Malachi smiled to himself. Once again, rousing Roger’s anger countered the man's fear. "Then there won't be a problem. I need time to think, and that would be best done on the walk back from here. Time *alone*. If you arrive before me, start unloading the boat and bringing things up to the cottage. And then when we're both there, we'll talk."

"Okay." Roger held up his hands for another item.

That ended the debate. They finished loading the rowboat and Roger immediately started untying it from the dock. "You'll be there soon," he said, the only indication that his fear hadn't completely been resolved.

"I will. You have my word." Malachi picked up the cart handles. "Be careful. If you arrive before me, start unloading. Bring things up to the verandah, and I'll sort them when I get there. If you aren't at the cottage when I arrive, I'll take your boat and find you."

"Might take a bit longer by water," Roger pointed out. "Won't be able to row as fast as this morning with all this stuff. You might beat me there."

"I'll still come looking." If nothing else, the words would reassure Roger that Malachi wouldn't desert him.

"Okay. See you."

To ensure that the man who'd confronted him didn't return or send anyone else who might recognize Roger, Malachi stayed where he was until Roger had rowed away from the dock. Once the other man was far enough into the harbor to be safe, Malachi pulled the cart back to the shop. He gave the grocer an additional dollar to thank him for the use of the cart and complimented the man on what a helpful worker his son was, then left.

As he walked out of town, his tension trickled away, though it didn't completely leave him. The encounter with the man at the dock had been far too close. At any moment, he might have sounded an alarm to the others in the boat shop. Roger's street wisdom had saved them as much as anything Malachi had said. The younger man had kept his head down, face hidden, and hadn't spoken. He'd recognized the danger more than Malachi had.

I should tell him that. He doubted Roger had heard much praise in his miserable existence. He should hear some now.

Half a mile outside the town limits, Malachi found a secluded spot and stripped off his clothes. He would have to leave them behind. The only way to carry them would be in his mouth, and he needed that free in case he had to defend himself or scare off a curious human by baring his teeth. But he had other clothing at home and could return later to retrieve these, if a scavenger didn't take them first. For that matter, there were plenty who might need the clothes more than he. Perhaps he would simply leave them for any who could benefit.

Shifting was an agonizing process. Malachi despised it, even at times like this when it was necessary for his sanity. He shifted much faster than most, from what he'd been told, so rapidly that to an outsider he appeared a man in one breath and a wolf the next. But the pain inherent in shifting compacted into a flare more intense than the shift itself, becoming a burning torment as skin, bones, and muscle all reshaped themselves from human to wolf. It was more than Malachi in his pre-shifter life would have been able to bear. Many times, he'd tried to prevent it entirely. But denying the shift was impossible. Once begun, it couldn't be stopped.

After a moment, Malachi stood in the space as a large, light grey wolf. Larger than most dogs, but small enough to pass as one if a human didn't look closely enough.

He knew where home was, and he ran through woods and fields, past a few houses. He saw no humans, only evidence that they existed. That suited him. He had no time for humans. Wind ruffled his fur and he reveled in it, in the scents carried on the breeze, in the feeling of movement faster than any human could manage.

He ran, and the running was all that mattered.

On four legs at full pace, reaching the turn-off to the cottage took far less time than it would have walking as a man. He wanted to keep running, maybe down to the far end of the island and back. That would be good, and there would be even less chance of meeting humans.

But he retained enough human reasoning to stop himself. He couldn't judge how much time had passed. Roger might already have returned. If he hadn't yet, he would shortly, and if Malachi wasn't present, Roger might worry. The man was already frightened. Malachi had no wish to add to it. He ran down the dirt road to the cottage. Surveying the beach below and water beyond, he saw no sign that Roger had arrived. That was good. He had time to shift back and recover.

He stopped short of the cottage to make the return shift. Reverting to human form always hurt worse than shifting into wolf, as the bones and body compacted into the smaller shape, but at least it took as little time. Once back in human form, he lay on the ground, ignoring the dirt and evergreen needles. His breathing was rapid and his body didn't want to cooperate with his attempts to rise. This happened every time he shifted and, while annoying, it didn't disturb him. He was concerned only because each moment he lay there made it more likely Roger would find him, and he wasn't prepared to explain to the other man why he lay nude outside the cottage.

He heard the slapping of oars against water below and forced himself to his feet. He had lost track of time, and now Roger was approaching. Cursing himself and his wolf, Malachi hurried into the cottage and yanked on a pair of trousers and a shirt as quickly as he could manage with his still-uncoordinated hands.

The cottage door opened and closed, and he left the bedroom to see Roger standing in the kitchen with a sack slung onto his shoulder. The other man looked confused. "You decided to change your clothes?"

"I slipped and fell on a patch of mud on the way home." The lie tumbled easily from Malachi's lips. "You made good time."

"You still got here first," Roger pointed out. "Where should I put this?"

"Just on the floor for now. We'll unload the boat and then I'll sort things into their places."

He remained barefoot while he and Roger brought the

provisions up from the boat. Still recovering from his shift, he found bare feet preferable to footwear. Particularly since his most comfortable shoes were miles back with the rest of his clothes. He would have to find a reason to go back for them, one Roger wouldn't question.

Or I could tell him the truth. He'll see for himself soon enough.

He said nothing to Roger while they made their trips back and forth. Once everything was in the kitchen, Malachi sat down in his favorite chair in the main room and stared out at the harbor as exhaustion struck him. He generally recovered from shifting without issue, but two shifts in less than an hour, on a day when he was still fending off the aftereffects of alcohol and worry, had done for him.

"Are you all right?" Roger sat on the small bench in front of the fireplace. "Walked too fast? You're breathing hard, and your face is dead white."

"I'll be fine." Malachi gave him a faint smile. "I may have gone a bit too fast. It isn't cause for concern."

"I can fix you some coffee or something." Roger glanced at the kitchen. "Food? Tell me what you need. I want to help you."

"I just need to sit for a little while." Malachi reconsidered. Shifting used a great deal of energy, and his stomach was grinding on itself. "There's bread in the breadbox, and the pan I used this morning is still in the sink. Fry some of the bread and we'll make a lunch of it for now."

"Sure." Roger scrambled to his feet and went into the kitchen. "Water? I mean, do you want some?"

"Yes. Thank you." He didn't bother telling Roger where the glasses were. He doubted Roger would have difficulty finding them on the open shelf above the sink.

He closed his eyes and listened to Roger bustling about in the kitchen. A sound he hadn't heard since childhood, when his mother had been the one preparing meals and drinks. He hadn't realized until now how much he missed having someone there to do things for him, not because they had to but just because they wanted to. Because that was part of making a home.

Foolishness.

The creaking floorboards heralded Roger's return to the main room before he softly said, "Malachi?"

"I'm awake." Malachi opened his eyes and took the glass of water that Roger held out to him. "Thank you. Listen, I had a thought." He might be considered an idiot for expressing it, but he spoke anyway. "You said you and Jonathan need a better life than you have now. That you'd thought of going west, but you'd need more money for that than you're able to obtain. There's more than enough room here for three, as you said yourself. Instead of going west, why not stay here?"

"With you?" Roger's expression, open and trusting until now, immediately closed to suspicion. "Why would you suggest that?"

"I'm starting to think I don't like being alone," Malachi answered as honestly as he could. "And I don't like the thought of you and him returning to the streets after this. You might be able to make your way out west, but it would be a dangerous trip. I have money. You can ask for work with the fishermen in town, either Lunenburg or Mahone Bay, and live here with me meanwhile."

He held his breath. He knew how he sounded: desperate and lonely. Roger was clearly neither accustomed nor willing to accept help from others, and given his protectiveness of Jonathan, he would likely be skeptical of Malachi's reasons for the offer. But the words were out now, and he couldn't take them back.

"Why?" Roger asked again. "You liked fucking us so much you want to keep doing it?"

"It doesn't have anything to do with that." Though that added to the appeal of having the two humans around. He certainly wouldn't mind a repeat of what they'd done on the beach. "Look, has no one ever offered to help you without wanting something from you?"

"Nope." Roger folded his arms. "You're helping us now, getting Jonathan away from the rumrunners. At least, you will be if you keep your word. I already wonder what you want for doing that."

"I want to know that he's safe," Malachi said. "That both of you are. You saved Jonathan from being beaten, right? You did things I can't even conceive of to support him so he wouldn't resort to those means himself. Did you do that so he'd let you fuck him?"

"Of course not! I told you, I waited for him two years. I wanted him to do it because he wanted, not because he owed me." Roger's glared deepened. "I don't know what you think of me, but I ain't like them!"

Malachi didn't need to ask whom Roger meant by "them." The scorn that dripped from the man's voice made it all too clear. "Nor am I," he said calmly. "I apologized for yesterday, didn't I? I wasn't thinking clearly. I saw you and Jonathan together and I let my cock lead me instead of my reason." He didn't mention the alcohol, though that more than anything had been responsible for his actions. Roger wouldn't have understood how he could have gotten drunk from a smell.

"And I told you I didn't mind it. Truth be told, I liked having your cock in me while I fucked him. Done it before. That's why I offered you to join in. I knew I'd like it." He chuckled. "Knew you were watching and that you'd have a stiff prick from what you saw. I thought I might as well offer you some relief since I was part of the cause of it."

"I shouldn't have watched you to begin with." Malachi sipped his water. "You and Jonathan deserved privacy, not a stranger viewing and taking part. As I said, I wasn't thinking clearly."

"You don't owe me no apology." Roger relaxed, but only slightly. "I fell for Jonathan. I ain't ashamed to say so. That's why I helped him and didn't ask him for anything. What's your reason?"

"Let's call it friendship for now." Malachi didn't believe in "falling for" someone so quickly. Lust could certainly be instantaneous, and friendships could form rapidly especially when forged by a situation like their current one. To Malachi, love required more time.

He wasn't falling for Jonathan or Roger, but he did care for them, despite how illogical it seemed. And he wanted them to remain with him.

"So you wouldn't expect anything?" Roger abruptly knelt in front of Malachi and fumbled at the fastenings on his trousers. "You wouldn't ask for this?"

"Stop." Malachi grabbed the other man's wrists. "No, I wouldn't ask. If you offered, I doubt I'd say no, but I wouldn't want you here just for an easy fuck. You don't believe me, and after what you told me of your past, I can't blame you a bit, but I am telling you the truth. I don't want anything from you or Jonathan. I just want to know you're safe. And I admit it would be nice not to be alone anymore."

"You're touched in the head." Roger looked up at him, and Malachi saw in the man's eyes how much he wanted to believe Malachi's words. His sad life had taken away hope. Roger had learned too early that he had to trade himself for anything that was offered. Malachi's heart nearly broke for what this young man had gone through.

"I'm not touched." He stood and pulled Roger to his feet. Still holding the other man's hands, he said, "Sometimes people just do things because they want to. I don't want anything from you except friendship. Any more than that, it's your choice to give or not. The same goes for Jonathan. If you stay, you and he can share a room if you like and have your love affair, and I'll leave you be unless you invite me. I won't touch either of you unless one or both of you ask. You have my word."

Roger opened and closed his mouth a few times before tears began to trickle down his cheeks. He tried to speak again, but managed only a sob. Instinctively, Malachi pulled the younger man into an embrace, and Roger cried in earnest, shaking as he let out over a decade of pain.

Malachi knew nothing comforting to say, so he didn't even try. He just held Roger, letting him know as best he could that everything would be all right, that Malachi wouldn't abandon him or think less of him.

Gradually Roger quieted, and finally he pulled away. "I'm sorry. I said I'd cook for you, and here I'm sniveling all over you instead."

"You had reason." Without thinking, Malachi brushed a lock of hair away from Roger's eye, a tender gesture he wouldn't have expected of himself. "Never mind the food, unless you're hungry too. I didn't even think. You can't have slept last night. You must be exhausted. The bedroom straight through there—" he pointed to the curtain that shielded the doorway of his childhood bedroom—"hasn't got any linens on the bed, but there's a blanket on the closet shelf you can cover up with. I'll wake you when it's time to go after Jonathan."

"I..." Roger trailed off, glancing between the curtain and Malachi. "Alone?"

"Of course, unless you don't want to be."

"Could you...?" Again he let his words run out. He sniffed and swallowed hard before trying again. "I know it sounds stupid. Like a baby. But could you lie down with me? I don't want to fuck. I just want—Hell, I don't know what I want."

From the man's inability to finish his thoughts, Malachi filled in the blank. "You want me to hold you? Like I was doing just now?"

Roger hesitated, then nodded. "Yeah. Like that. No one except Jonathan and my mother have ever done that, and my mother stopped after Dad died. She said I had to be the man then, and men didn't need hugs and cuddles."

"She's wrong. I think everyone needs those." God knew he did, and he had no one to give it to him. Until now. "I don't think it's childish at all, and I don't mind it if it's what you want. Go in and lie down. I need to eat something before I come in."

"I'd rather wait." Roger sat on the fireplace bench again. "I don't like just walking into someone's room."

"It's a vacant room."

"I'll wait," Roger repeated.

Deciding that arguing would be pointless, Malachi went into the kitchen and quickly ate a few slices of bread, which he washed down with an apple from the collection of provisions still scattered around the room. After he got Roger to sleep, he would put things away while he waited for nightfall.

When he finished his meal, such as it was, Malachi found Roger nearly asleep on the bench. He helped the other man to his feet and into the small bedroom, where he made Roger sit on the edge of the bed. “Take off your shoes. I’ll get the blanket.”

“I’m not cold.” Roger bent to untie his shoes.

“You might want it later.” Malachi went to the closet and found the handwoven blanket he’d slept with every night that he’d spent in this cottage until leaving for university. His grandmother had made it for him. She’d passed away shortly after his change, and one of his biggest regrets was avoiding her funeral. He’d been too afraid of questions from family to risk attending.

“Lie down,” he said to Roger.

Roger did so, moving over toward the wall to leave room for Malachi. The narrow bed scarcely had room for two grown men, but Malachi lay beside Roger and the two of them squirmed and maneuvered until Malachi was able to comfortably embrace the younger man.

“This is nice,” Roger murmured.

“I agree.” Malachi fought a sudden urge to kiss Roger, mindful of his promise not to touch him unless asked. This sentimentality was unfamiliar to Malachi, and he wasn’t sure how to navigate it, especially with another man.

“Jonathan and I wouldn’t be able to share this,” Roger said. “He kicks in his sleep.”

“There’s a third room with a larger bed,” Malachi said. “It’s cluttered now, but we could clean it out. I left this room empty instead of that one because this was mine when I was young. The other belonged to my parents until they passed.”

Roger yawned. “Don’t know why, but I feel safe like this. Like nothing and no one can hurt me no more.”

“I won’t let you be hurt.” Malachi wondered at himself for speaking the words. He meant them, but hadn’t intended to say them.

"I know."

That was the last thing Roger said. After a few moments, a quiet snore broke the silence. Malachi smiled and eased away from Roger. In sleep, the man looked softer, more innocent. The way he might have been if his life hadn't been destroyed by those who chose to mistreat him.

Malachi vowed to himself that if Roger and Jonathan chose to stay with him, he would make certain they were never mistreated again.

CHAPTER FOUR

WHILE Roger slept, Malachi put away his provisions, storing some in the ice box and the small pantry off the kitchen and the rest in the cold closet his father had built beneath the cottage. He worked as quietly as he could, not wanting to wake Roger until the man had at least a few hours of solid sleep. How Roger had managed the morning's trip, and especially the row back from Lunenburg followed by carrying all the purchases uphill to the cottage, was beyond him. He must have run purely on willpower and coffee.

After he finished that task, Malachi prepared another meal for himself and ate it seated in his chair, looking out the picture window at the bay. He missed the sails which often dotted the water during the summer months. For long stretches of days, they reminded him that he wasn't entirely alone. That people were nearby if he chose to speak to them. He had never made that choice, afraid as he was of being found by other werewolves or discovered by humans. But the sails reminded him of the possibility.

Now, between the coolness of the weather and the Depression, which had necessitated many people selling off frivolous belongings like sailboats, the bay was empty. Lonely, as Malachi himself had often felt and had denied until now. It had taken two petty criminals, one naïve and one broken, to show him what he'd lacked by hiding himself away for so long.

As the sun began to set, he went into the small bedroom and knelt beside the bed. Somewhere in the intervening time, Roger had pulled the blanket over himself, and now he lay on his side curled up like a young boy, breathing deeply and evenly, with a small smile on his face. Happy dreams, Malachi hoped.

He hated to wake the other man, but it was nearly time to leave. And before they went, he had to explain to Roger what would happen. All of it. Including Malachi's shifting.

"Roger?" He spoke softly, hoping not to startle the man.

Roger's eyes immediately opened, and he backed away from Malachi until his back was against the wall. Clearly he didn't immediately recall where he was. "It's all right," Malachi said in a tone he hoped would prove soothing. "It's me, Malachi. You're in my cottage, and we have to get ready to go after Jonathan. Do you remember?"

"Yeah. Yeah." Roger stretched and sat up. "Okay. It's time?"

"Almost. I need to talk to you about something first." He could only hope the discussion would go well. Or at least that Roger wouldn't run away from the insane man who claimed to be a werewolf.

"Can I have coffee while you talk?"

"Of course." Malachi stood. "I'll fix it. Come to the main room when you're ready."

He went into the kitchen. While he waited for water to boil, he tried to plan his explanation. Most humans had heard of werewolves. They just didn't believe weres existed outside of stories. Roger would be skeptical at best. Malachi's chore was to convince the other man of what he actually was. If necessary, he could shift to prove the truth, but that would frighten Roger more than he wanted to risk.

Roger came out of the bedroom and stumbled through the kitchen and out the door. It took Malachi a moment to figure out why the other man had gone outside. He'd forgotten to mention the indoor toilet to his guest.

Roger re-entered several seconds later, rubbing his eyes.

"No outhouse?"

"In there." Malachi pointed to the door a few feet beyond the fireplace.

"Rich people." Roger staggered into the room, leaving the door open. Malachi prudently ignored it and the sounds which emerged.

After a moment, Roger returned to the kitchen and leaned against the counter. "It's nearly dark. We can leave now."

"You need your coffee, and I need to explain the plan to you." Malachi handed the man the coffee he'd prepared.

Roger sipped the hot beverage and looked warily at Malachi over the rim of the cup. Malachi took a deep breath. "We'll be able to get him out, but you have to trust me. And you have to do what I say. Will you do that?"

"If it means saving Jonathan, I'll do almost anything." Roger set the cup on the counter. "Talk fast, because I'm about to leave without you."

"First rule, stay with me unless I tell you otherwise." Malachi ran his hand through his hair. "Listen. This is going to be hard to believe. If you think I've gone mad, you can walk away, but I promise everything I'm about to say is the truth. I'm risking my own life by telling you any of this, so I hope you'll at least hear me out before you make any judgments."

"That don't sound too good." Folding his arms, he looked directly into Malachi's eyes. Malachi, to his surprise, had to look away. "Go on."

"The men in that shed wouldn't likely be afraid of the two of us as we are now." Malachi walked into the living room, where he had more room to pace. The more nervous he became, the more he needed to move. For the moment, though, he managed to stand still.

Roger followed him and sat at the dining table. "They ain't afraid of anyone except the bosses," he said. "I didn't figure we were going to waltz in and tell them to give Jonathan back."

"We aren't. In fact, you aren't going in at all until you hear the signal." Now he had no choice but to tell Roger everything.

Fortunately, just beginning to talk about it started his mind working. “I’ll tell you in a minute what the signal will be.”

“You’re going in there alone?” Roger raised his eyebrows. “You are mad.”

“No. I’m a werewolf.”

He spoke the words simply and matter-of-factly because there was no other way. He could have danced around the subject, but that would only have wasted time. Now the truth was out. Roger might walk away. The others might somehow find out that Malachi had told and come to kill him, especially if they already sought to do so. No matter. He had told the truth, and he was neither able nor willing to take it back.

For seconds that stretched to eternities, Roger just sat at the table, one hand on his cup, staring at Malachi. Malachi wanted to look away, to focus on anything except the man he’d begun to care for so deeply, but he forced himself to meet Roger’s gaze. Looking away now would be as good as admitting he’d lied. Or admitting he expected Roger to reject him.

“You’re a werewolf,” Roger said slowly.

Relieved that the silence had been broken, Malachi nodded. “I was attacked several years ago, one night while I was in university. I brought a girl—we were engaged—here to the cottage for a weekend alone. No one knew we were here. We ended up in the wrong place at the wrong time.”

“Right. Being bitten by a werewolf makes you one.” Roger snorted. “Are you trying to make me think you’re crazy so I’ll leave? So you don’t have to help me?”

“No. I want you to stay. I told you that.” Malachi fidgeted but refused to allow himself to pace. “I know it sounds insane at best, Roger. That’s exactly what I thought when I was told what I was. The only reason I believed it was that I’d awakened in wolf form. When you’re attacked, you automatically shift to wolf so you can recover.”

“Sure you do.” Roger crossed one leg over the other. “I don’t know if you’re lying on purpose or you really believe what you’re saying. I don’t think I can believe it.”

"I won't blame you if you don't," Malachi said. "This is the plan to save Jonathan, though. The rumrunners won't be afraid of two men. They'll be afraid of a wolf."

Roger licked his upper lip, a movement that appeared more nervous than anything. "Can you show me? I seen a movie once with a werewolf. Didn't look like anything more than a man in a wolf suit, but that was a movie. Can you show me that you're not making this up?"

Malachi sighed. He had hoped to avoid shifting again so soon. His plan had been to wait until he reached the spot where he'd shifted earlier and take wolf form there. If he acceded to Roger's request, he would have to travel all the way to Lunenburg as a wolf, because he would be unable to cope with multiple shifts in such a short time. But having Roger believe and accept what he was would be well worth the price. "I will as soon as we finish going over the plan. Once I change to wolf form, I'm going to have to stay that way until we come back here with Jonathan, and I won't be able to talk to you."

"Fair enough." Roger's eyes glinted, and Malachi realized that despite his skepticism—or perhaps because of it—the other man was amused. "So you're going to be a werewolf and run in and terrify them?"

"Essentially." Clearly Roger wasn't taking this seriously, but Malachi would just have to accept that for the time being. He had the basic gist, at least. "Werewolves don't look like what they showed in that movie. When I change into wolf form, I look like a real wolf, though larger than a natural wolf would be."

"So what's going to scare them, then?"

"Teeth."

Roger paused as that sank in. "Okay. You run in and terrify them because you look like a real wolf with sharp teeth? And then what do I do?"

"I'll distract them," Malachi said. "And if I don't see Jonathan right away, I'll keep moving myself and the men until I find him. When you hear me howl—and believe me, you will hear it—follow the sound to where I am. That's where Jonathan will be.

I'll keep the men away from you while you get Jonathan out."

"And how are we going to get back here? I guess werewolves can't row boats."

Malachi had to chuckle at that. "I can't even get into a rowboat in wolf form. The boat would be weighed down too much."

He sobered as he pondered Roger's question. He'd settled how to get to Lunenburg himself, but he'd neglected the logistics of how Roger would get there and bring Jonathan back. In darkness, rowing between Herman's Island and Lunenburg could be dangerous. Malachi had done it before, and despite his familiarity with the waters he'd nearly run aground. Roger didn't know the waters.

Somehow, though, he'd managed to find his way to Malachi that morning, and it must have been still dark when he'd left town. Perhaps he could navigate it.

Despite the danger, on the water, Roger and Jonathan might be safer. The rumrunners wouldn't want to risk their boats pursuing a couple of petty thieves. Even if they did, Roger and Jonathan would have more opportunity to escape and hide. "Do you think you can row between here and town in the dark without me guiding you? I'll have to go by road and woods and meet you there."

The other man looked uncertain but nodded. "Made it from there to here this morning before full sunrise. I think I can do it. So the plan is for me to get Jonathan out and into the boat?"

"You'll tie up where we did this morning," Malachi said. "Wait till I'm on the dock before you come, though. Otherwise they might see you before I arrive."

"Okay."

"You'll have to explain to Jonathan who I am." The last thing Malachi wanted was for the young man to be so frightened he couldn't move. "But you'll have to do it on the run."

"I can manage Jonathan. He trusts me." Roger shook his head. "If I find out you're making this up or you've gone insane, I'll kill you. You know that?"

"I know." He didn't doubt it for a moment. "Come outside and I'll prove it to you. And then you'll have to leave right away. I run faster than you can row, and if I'm in town too long waiting for you, someone might capture me."

"Then run slower." Roger stood and drank more of his coffee, then put the cup in the kitchen sink. "Come on."

"One moment." Malachi stripped off his trousers. Roger's eyes widened. "I can't change in clothing," Malachi explained. "They don't fit well when I'm a wolf."

"Of course." Roger licked his lips again. This time the move seemed more seductive. "Sure you don't want a bit of relief first?"

"Aren't you the one in a hurry to save your lover?"

"Yeah." Roger grinned. "Afterward, then." He spun on one heel and went outside.

Shaking his head, Malachi followed, thankful as always that at this time of year there were no neighbors to see him nude. He walked several feet away from the cottage, closed his eyes, and brought his wolf to the fore.

As always, the shift was painful. His awareness of being watched by a human only increased his discomfort. He tried to pretend this was a shift like any other, but Roger's gaze was nearly tangible.

Finally he lay on the ground, panting through an elongated mouth, head between his two front paws. Only then did he open his eyes and look at Roger.

The man's mouth was open and his eyes were wide. Malachi smelled fear, and he liked it. He remembered who this man was, though. This was a friend, and they wouldn't hurt each other. He didn't want the man's fear, only his trust.

"Holy Mary." Roger took a deep breath. "You meant it. Christ."

Malachi, of course, couldn't respond. He pushed himself to his feet and slowly approached the man. Roger stood his ground, though the scent of fear increased as Malachi came close enough to touch his snout to Roger's hand.

"You won't hurt me," Roger said, sounding more certain than his trembling would have led Malachi to believe.

With no other way to answer, Malachi licked Roger's hand as a dog might. Roger's face broke into a smile. "Nah, you won't hurt me. Okay. I believe you, and if you can be as scary as you said, I think we'll have Jonathan back soon. I'm leaving now, like you said. I'll stay away from the dock in town until I see you on it."

Malachi nodded. Roger tentatively patted Malachi's head before turning to go down to the boats.

Malachi waited until the slap of oars against water told him that Roger was underway. Then he ran.

He went fast but didn't go directly to town. He had time to give himself a bit of freedom, and he took that time. The tiny human part of him that remained when he turned wolf was frightened, nervous about rescuing the blond man. He needed to run, to forget that he existed as anything other than wolf.

The run exhilarated him. Only at times like this, the rare times he allowed himself to just go, did he truly feel alive. He stayed in woods, so he had no fear of being seen. He didn't think. He just moved and let the wind in his fur remind him that he had a reason to exist. The sounds of trees and water filled his ears. After his change and his choice to leave the pack that had taken him in, he had disconnected himself from everyone and everything. In wolf form, surrounded only by nature, he felt connected. It was the closest to happiness that he had in his life.

Finally, though, he had no choice but to enter Lunenburg. He slowed once he passed the first house inside the town limits. A running wolf would attract more attention than one that walked or trotted. If humans spotted him, it would be very bad.

He made his way to the harbor without seeing anyone and stopped at the street end of the dock where he'd told Roger to tie up. Out on the water, not quite into the harbor yet but nearly there, Roger rowed quickly toward him.

Malachi stood completely still and waited until Roger reached the dock. For Malachi, time didn't matter. He didn't mind the wait. But when Roger reached the top of the ladder he looked frantic. “We have to hurry. It’s late.”

Malachi simply turned and trotted toward the front of the boat shop. Roger had to remember the plan. If he entered the shop before Malachi had the humans under control, they might be caught. Malachi wasn’t concerned about himself. He could fight anyone. But he didn’t know whether he would be able to free both Jonathan and Roger if it came to it.

The shop door stood open, letting the cool fall air into the building. Malachi walked in as if he belonged there, and was halfway into the large space where boats were built in better times, and where crates of hooch stood now, before anyone noticed him.

A whistle pierced the air. Malachi winced at the sharp sound. “Look at that dog. He’s a beaut!”

“That ain’t a dog.” The stocky man who had offered to help Malachi load his boat earlier walked over and stared at Malachi. Malachi averted his eyes, not because the man was dominant but because he himself was. Men were fools sometimes. They knew no better than to stare a wolf in the eye. Malachi didn’t want a dominance fight with a human. It couldn’t end well.

“What the hell is it, then?” the first man who had spoken asked.

“Looks like a wolf.” The stocky man crouched in front of Malachi. “Seen a few when I went out west last year.”

“There ain’t wolves in Lunenburg.” A third man walked over. “Chase it out. We have work to do. Have to get that shipment out before dawn or there’ll be hell to pay.”

“Let me help you. It’ll get done quicker.”

Malachi recognized that voice, and he yearned to see the face of the man who had spoken. The blond man. The one he was here to rescue. The one who was in his heart.

He leaned to one side and saw Jonathan, tied to a chair with knots any child with a fisherman father would have been able to undo. He started toward the young man, but the stocky one blocked him. “No, doggy. Go back home.”

Malachi growled low in his throat. He refused to be chased,

and he was damned if he would be insulted. But the stocky man's attempt to stop him reminded him that he wasn't here to see Jonathan. He had to get these men out of the way so Roger could enter. Malachi could do many things, but untying knots without hands wasn't one of them.

He stalked toward the man who had blocked him. That man stood his ground for a second, until Malachi growled again. Then he backed up. "Chase it off."

The third man, the one who had told them to get back to work, approached. Malachi turned his head for a second and bared his teeth, and that man stepped back so quickly he fell on his ass. "Thing's rabid, Hugh. Got to be."

"No foam." Hugh, the stocky man, stepped forward again. "Come on, you. Out of here."

"I'm good with animals," Jonathan said. "Untie me and I'll chase him out for you."

A fourth man, whom Malachi hadn't seen until now, suddenly stepped in front of Jonathan and smacked him across the face. "Shut up, you. Think we're idiots? You're staying right there till your friend comes back."

That did it. Malachi would not see Jonathan hurt. He lunged past the three men and ran to knock the fourth to the floor. The other three ran to them, shouting words Malachi didn't try to comprehend as he lowered his teeth to the fourth man's throat.

"No!"

If any of the rumrunners had shouted, Malachi would have ignored them. He would have ripped out the throat of the man beneath him, either killing him or changing him. He wouldn't have cared which.

But it was Jonathan's voice, and that got through. One of the things Malachi had learned during his time with the pack was the shifter law against attacking humans. He could hold the man on the floor as long as he needed, but if he scratched or, worse, bit, the man he would break that law. And deep inside, he didn't want to harm any of these men. He only wanted to free Jonathan.

He stopped with his teeth just barely touching the skin on

the man's neck. The man whimpered but stayed still. The other three stood around like they didn't know what to do, which was fine with Malachi. He was there to distract them. As long as they were trying to figure out how to get him off their pal, they weren't paying attention to Jonathan.

Raising his head, he howled.

Then there was chaos. Roger ran in. Hugh spotted him first and yelled at the other two to grab him. Roger dodged them, but he was outnumbered until Malachi decided to let go of the guy he was holding down. He knocked the skinnier of Roger's pursuers to the ground and pretended to bite him, which attracted everyone's attention except Roger's.

Keeping the men away from Roger and Jonathan took all Malachi's focus. He was barely aware of the two men—*his* two men—fleeing the shop. Only when he heard Roger shout, "Now!" from outside did he leave the men he'd been menacing. They followed him to the door, but when he whirled around and snarled at them they fell back. Roger's call hopefully meant that he and Jonathan were safely in the rowboat on their way back to the cottage, but Malachi didn't want to take any chances on the rumrunners giving chase before Roger and Jonathan had a solid head start.

When he judged that enough time had passed, he turned and ran. This time, the rumrunners didn't follow.

Malachi headed straight back to the cottage. It might take time for Roger and Jonathan to arrive, but he would need that time to shift back and recover. He didn't know what had been done to Jonathan in the boat shop, other than the blow he'd witnessed, but he suspected that being tied to a chair for hours would leave Jonathan stiff and sore even if nothing else had occurred. He would need to be in human form to help Jonathan into the cottage. Not to mention avoiding scaring the hell out of the man.

He shifted outside the cottage and limped inside to put on his clothes. His stomach rumbled, reminding him that he needed food again. Reasoning that Roger and Jonathan might be hungry as well, he fried the eggs that were left, along with the remaining bread and some sausages he'd purchased in town that morning. By the time the food was ready, he heard voices from the beach. Roger must have strained himself to his limits to make such rapid time from town to here.

Malachi grabbed a too-hot sausage and devoured it before he reached the slope to the beach. He needed more food to rebuild his strength, but first he had to make sure Jonathan and Roger were all right.

The boat steered straight toward him, and he stepped into the water to pull it up onto the sand. His arms and legs ached, but he ignored the pain. It would pass. It always did.

Jonathan sat slumped in the bow of the boat, eyes closed. His eyelids fluttered but didn't open when Malachi touched his shoulder.

"Is either of you hurt?" Malachi asked, looking at Jonathan though he spoke to Roger.

"Fucking arms hurt like hell." Roger set the oars on the bottom of the boat and stepped out of it. "Won't be able to move them tomorrow, likely. I didn't know if they were after us or not."

"I doubt they were. They didn't dare leave the shop while I was there." Malachi gently shook Jonathan. Again his eyelids fluttered. "Is he asleep or unconscious?"

"Some of both, I think. You scared him half to death." Roger knelt on the sand beside the boat. "Jonny, we're safe now. Come on. We can't carry you. You have to get out of the boat now."

"No," Jonathan moaned.

"Jonathan, wake up," Malachi said.

He spoke gently but firmly, and just as Jonathan's cry in the boat shop had gotten through to him, now his words got through to the younger man. Jonathan opened his eyes and looked around before fixing his gaze on Malachi's face. "We're back here?"

"Yes, and we don't want to stay long on the beach." Malachi reached out a hand, and Jonathan took it. "If I help you up, can you stand?"

"Don't know. I think so." Jonathan allowed Malachi to pull him to his feet. Roger quickly moved to support his friend as Jonathan carefully stepped out of the boat. "Been sitting since last night. My legs are all tingly. And I…" He trailed off and looked around. "It isn't here, is it? That wolf from the shop?"

"We'll talk about that later." Malachi caught Roger's eye and gave him a warning look. Roger nodded. Jonathan would need to know the truth eventually, but not yet. Right now, the younger man needed food and rest.

They walked side-by-side on a path barely wide enough for two men, never mind three. Jonathan's legs shook visibly, and Malachi wasn't willing to risk him falling and injuring himself. He and Roger both supported Jonathan, who kept one arm around each of them until they reached the cottage.

"Settle him in my chair," Malachi directed Roger as they entered the cottage. "I have food. I think we can forego the table this once. He'll need to put his feet up. There's a stool under the window."

Roger obeyed, slowly leading his lover into the main room while Malachi took down three plates and divided the food he'd cooked among them. He gave himself the largest share, quelling a pang of guilt by reminding himself that he'd exerted himself more than either of the other men could understand and he needed the fuel to keep his body functioning.

He brought Jonathan's share first and watched until the man picked up a slice of bread and bit off a piece before returning to the kitchen for the other two plates. Roger sat again on the fireplace bench, the closest seat to Jonathan, and he started eating without taking his eyes off his friend.

Malachi sat at the table but turned his chair to face the other two. "I have water and juice as well," he said. "You'll both need to drink something, but I need to eat before I serve anything else."

"I'll get the drinks." Roger set his plate on the bench and scrambled into the kitchen. Water ran in the sink, out of Malachi's view behind the wall that separated the rooms, and Roger returned a few seconds later carrying two glasses. He gave one to Jonathan and the other to Malachi and went back into the kitchen for his own.

"This is good." Jonathan spoke through a mouthful of egg. He didn't eat as ravenously as Roger had earlier, but Malachi suspected he was at least as hungry. Possibly more so. Neither of these men had had enough to eat recently, if ever.

Jonathan swallowed and looked at Malachi. "How'd you know Roger was bringing me here?"

"I came to him this morning after they said they were keeping you." Roger sat on the bench again and picked up his plate, but didn't eat. "You said he told you to come back if we needed help, so I did."

"Why didn't he help you, then?" Jonathan demanded. "You came for me alone."

Roger looked at Malachi. Malachi nodded. It was time for Jonathan to know the truth.

"He was there," Roger said.

"Didn't see him," Jonathan argued.

"Yes, you did." Malachi set down his fork. His stomach was in knots. Telling Roger the truth had gone better than he'd expected, and he hoped that would be the case now as well. But he didn't know how Jonathan would take the news, and he was afraid to find out. "You saw me knock down the man who hit you."

"Someone hit him?" Roger's voice hardened. "Wish I'd known."

"I dealt with him." Malachi kept his gaze on Jonathan. "You saw that."

"I saw a wolf." Jonathan wrinkled his brow. His confusion slowly gave way to wide eyes as he realized what Malachi was saying. "That isn't possible."

"It is," Roger said. "Saw him change myself. He's a werewolf, Jonny, like in that movie I told you about, remember?"

"That's a fucking movie!" Jonathan bent over as his yell gave way to a coughing fit. Roger quickly stood and took the plate off

Jonathan's lap and the glass from his hand. Several seconds passed before Jonathan reached for his food. Roger handed him the glass first and Jonathan sipped the water.

"That's pretty much how I felt about it at first," Roger said. He set the plate back on his friend's lap and returned to his seat. "Didn't choke, though. You okay?"

"Yeah." Jonathan drank more water. "You believe him?"

"I said I saw him change." Roger sounded a little impatient. "Why the hell else do you think a wolf showed up there? You think wolves just happen to wander around Lunenburg?"

"I can't listen to this." Jonathan stood and walked over to the table to set down his plate and glass. "Malachi, for whatever help you gave us, thanks. If you were the only one telling me you're a werewolf, I'd be running. Or calling for help, maybe. Roger believes you, and I trust him, but right now I can't hear this. I—" He pressed the heels of his hands against his eyes. "I can't."

"You're exhausted." Malachi wanted to comfort the man the way he had Roger, but under the circumstances he doubted Jonathan wanted his touch. "Jonathan, listen. Did they hurt you? Other than the man who hit you, did any of them lay a hand on you?"

He couldn't quite bring himself to say what he was truly asking. Jonathan seemed to understand anyway. He shook his head vehemently. "I would have killed them if they'd tried. They smacked me a few times, that's all."

"I'll kill them for *that*," Roger muttered.

"Let it pass," Malachi said. "Roger, the bed I mentioned is through this door." He pointed to the door beside the other end of the table. "You both ought to wash up a bit, but the world won't end if you're too tired to do so tonight. You'll need to clear the bed off, though, so it might be good to do that now. I think Jonathan needs rest."

"I do too, after all that damn rowing." Roger set his plate and glass beside Jonathan's and went into the bedroom.

Jonathan stayed where he was, swaying slightly on unsteady legs. "Sit down," Malachi said gently. "Whether I'm insane or a werewolf—or both—you have my word I won't hurt you. I promised you that yesterday."

"I know." Jonathan yanked the chair at the head of the table toward him and sat down. "How'd you get Roger to believe you? He don't trust anyone except me." He paused. "I don't even know if he trusts me."

"I do," Roger said from the bedroom. "And for the third time, I believe him because he changed into a wolf in front of me. I saw for myself, that's why."

"I can't change in front of you right now," Malachi said, anticipating Jonathan's question. "I've already turned wolf and back twice today. Once this morning and once just now. It uses me up, and I'm probably as exhausted as you are right now. Another shift today would leave me flat on my back for days."

"That could be fun, depending," Roger said.

"Hush." Malachi's face warmed.

Jonathan didn't miss the teasing. "Did you two…you know?"

"It's called fucking, Jonny." Roger came back into the room. "You're a grown man and you've done it. You can learn to say it. No, Malachi and I didn't fuck while you were gone. Just yesterday on the beach when I was fucking you."

Jonathan's face seemed to turn redder each time Roger repeated the word "fuck." Malachi found it cute, though it showed just how innocent the young man was. "It ain't like you and me own each other."

"Nope, but it ain't like I'm going to fuck someone just because they're there, either. Not now that I've had you." Roger rested his hand on Jonathan's shoulder. "I stopped doing that when I found you. Mostly." He shrugged. "I couldn't stop altogether. Too used to doing it, and I wanted to wait for you till you were ready. Plus I was paid for it. But now, if we're going to keep doing it, I promise I won't fuck anyone else. I don't want to."

Jonathan looked surprised. He bit his lip and nodded. "Should we talk about that now?"

"I can go into my room if that makes it easier," Malachi said. "I don't think anyone should talk about anything serious tonight.

You've been through a lot, Jonathan, and Roger was nearly mad worrying about you. Both of you should sleep. You can sort out everything else in the morning."

"I agree." Roger took Jonathan's arm and pulled him to his feet. "Come on, Jonny. Bed's big enough to share, and I promise we'll just sleep. Malachi's right. Everything will make more sense after we get some sleep."

Jonathan nodded. "You said something about washing up?"

"Through there." Malachi nodded toward the washroom door.

Jonathan went into the small room and closed the door. "Think I went too far with what I said?" Roger asked in a near whisper.

"I think the same thing I said before: save the discussion for morning." On impulse, Malachi put his arms around the other man. Roger relaxed into the embrace almost immediately. "He cares for you. A man doesn't expect to hear declarations of love from another man. He'll grow accustomed to it. I believe he wants the same thing you do, but he's still afraid of what people might think."

"And I'm not?" Roger pulled away and smiled mischievously. "It would be fun to have you flat on your back, you know. I mean to keep my promise to Jonathan, but if he agrees to it, I wouldn't mind another time like yesterday."

Malachi's cock stirred, and arousal ran through him. He had no excuse this time. No alcohol, no scene to stimulate him. Only desire for both men.

He shook his head and pushed the feeling away. "We're all going to sleep. I'm not going to talk about that now."

"But you want it. I can tell." Roger's grin broadened. "The offer's there if Jonathan says he don't mind. Just so's you know."

Jonathan emerged from the washroom and yawned. "You talking about me?"

"Just that you need some sleep." Roger went to his friend and put an arm around his shoulders. "Come on, I'll show you where we'll be. It's nicer than anywhere else we've slept, that's sure." He gave Malachi another teasing glance before leading Jonathan into the bedroom.

Just that look was enough to bring Malachi's cock to full hardness. He couldn't help the memories of fucking Roger while Roger was inside Jonathan. The images from the day before filled his mind and fueled his arousal. He rubbed himself through his trousers and wished he hadn't been so adamant about sending the younger men to bed.

He wished he had the confidence to join them. To ask for what he wanted.

But he had told Jonathan and Roger to sleep, and he needed to do the same. He put the dishes in the kitchen sink, intending to wash them in the morning. After quickly washing up in the washroom, he went into his room, stripped, and crawled under the blanket on his bed.

He ached, and not only from the shift. Though he tried to stop thinking about the men in the other room, his prick was still fully hard. He had trained himself to ignore lust for the most part. He had no outlet for it other than his own hand, and he didn't enjoy that as much as he might have if there had been alternatives.

But after several minutes of tossing and turning, he knew he would never sleep until he relieved the hunger Roger's teasing had roused. On his back, fully aware that was the position about which Roger had teased him, he wrapped one hand around his shaft and stroked.

He didn't focus his mind, merely allowed images to form. Jonathan's mouth on Roger's cock. His own cock inside Roger's ass. More images, ones that had yet to occur in reality: His mouth on Jonathan's shaft while Roger thrust into the blond man. Or while Roger thrust into Malachi, though he had never before considered allowing another man to take him.

It didn't matter whether he would ever allow it. The images were pure fantasy, and they rapidly brought him to the boiling point. He wanted both of the other men. Needed them. If either had given the slightest invitation, he would have gone to their bed now, but he forced himself to stay in his own bed, stroking himself harder and faster until he erupted onto his hand, grunting loudly, teeth clenched to keep from shouting.

As the pleasure faded, he lay panting, listening closely for any indication that the other men might have heard him. The entire main room lay between his bedroom and theirs, and their door was closed as was his, but he'd been louder than intended.

He heard nothing, though, so after a few moments he got up and wiped himself clean on the shirt he'd worn earlier, then lay down again. He fell asleep within minutes.

CHAPTER FIVE

LOUD banging on the cottage door jolted Malachi out of a sound, dreamless sleep. He sat bolt upright, heart pounding. Hearing the other bedroom door open, he rose quickly and hurried to his own door.

Jonathan stood beside the dining table, nude and wide-eyed. "It's them," he whispered. "The runners. They found us!"

"I'll deal with them." Malachi quickly pulled on the nearest pair of trousers, heedless of the fact that they needed washing. "Go back to your room. Tell Roger to stay there with you. Unless you hear the word..." He paused, trying to think of something he wouldn't be likely to say. "Shifter. Unless you hear me say shifter, both of you stay out of sight. Hear?"

"I hear." Jonathan backed into the bedroom. "You sure?"

"Do what I say and we'll be all right."

He crossed the main room as Jonathan closed the bedroom door. The visitor banged again on the front door, longer and louder this time. Malachi strode through the kitchen and yanked open the door with an expression he hoped telegraphed annoyance.

Three men stood there, one clothed in a law enforcement uniform. The other two, Malachi had seen in the boat shop: the man he'd knocked to the floor and the stocky one, Hugh.

Although the rumrunners were technically breaking the law, they would certainly have enough connections in town to allow them to contact the police without fear of being taken in themselves.

The nameless man took a step back. Hugh looked startled. The officer merely folded his arms. “Malachi Powers?”

“Yes.” Malachi squared his shoulders. “May I help you?”

“We’re looking for two men. Young, early twenties or so. One blond, one dark-haired.” The officer craned his neck to see past Malachi. “I believe we’ve found their boat down on your beach. Have you seen them?”

Malachi silently cursed himself for not insisting on hiding Roger and Jonathan’s boat. Outwardly, he kept his expression carefully neutral. “Have they done something wrong?”

“Stole from us,” Hugh said. “We just want our property back.”

From the hardness in the man’s eyes, Malachi suspected “property” extended to include Jonathan. He also suspected that coming here hadn’t been Hugh’s idea. The other man from the boat shop had seemed to have more authority than Hugh. He was probably one of the bosses Roger had mentioned. Most likely the one who had ordered Jonathan held while Roger was sent to bring back additional hooch.

An involuntary growl rose in Malachi’s throat, and he pressed his lips together to keep it from escaping. “The other cottages around here are empty. Are you sure they didn’t break into one? That would seem probable if they’re trying to hide.”

“Have you seen them or not?” the officer asked impatiently. “I haven’t got time for hunting, here.”

“I heard something in the Creightons’ cottage over there last night.” Malachi pointed toward the nearest cottage. “I’d check there if I were you.”

“I’ll go take a look.” The officer didn’t appear pleased, perhaps because he recognized that Malachi still hadn’t given him a straight answer. Nor would he. He was scarcely about to admit that Roger and Jonathan were in his cottage, and he refused to lie outright. This man would simply have to accept the answers he gave.

The officer motioned for Hugh and the other man to stay put, as Malachi had hoped. As soon as the officer was out of hearing, Malachi leaned closer to the other men. "I know who you are. I was at that shop last night."

"Only ones there besides us were a couple of our other men and the two crooks," Hugh said.

"And the wolf." Malachi looked directly into the man's eyes. "I heard he was more than a little frightening. And he can be dangerous. It wouldn't be wise to anger him."

He didn't state outright that he was the wolf, of course. Whatever the men inferred from his statement, he would not blatantly tell them what he was. That would be foolish at best. But he hoped the implication was clear.

The paleness of the unnamed man's face indicated that it was. "That thing almost bit me. You telling me it belongs to you?"

"In a sense." Malachi leaned forward even more. "You're brave to bring the police into this. Keep in mind that rumrunning's against the law, whether it's two young men who are just the end of a chain of smuggling or the bigger fish who bring the hooch into the States. You might find the men you're looking for, but they can give the police information you might not want them to give. If I were you, I'd write it off as a loss and move on with your lives."

"They stole from us," the pale man said. "I ain't the one they'll be answering to."

"What did they steal?" Malachi asked as if he didn't know.

"A jug of rum," the man replied. "Part of a shipment. The people waiting won't be happy to have their shipment short."

"One jug?" Malachi snorted, putting on an act. Let the man think he was insulting him. He thought it ridiculous that they were pursuing Roger and Jonathan for something so minor anyway, and he wasn't about to let the man believe he was in the right. "For one jug, you're risking your whole operation?"

"The cop's my cousin," Hugh said. "He won't turn on us."

"Everyone is everyone's cousin in Lunenburg," Malachi said. "You and I are more than likely related back along the line. I saw the men you're talking about when I was in town last night. They're kids. Probably got a little excited about having hooch so close and decided to test it out. You're going to chase them down for that?"

He was forming a plan, one he hoped would make this danger go away. Then he would only have to worry about the other werewolves finding out that he'd told humans about himself. Since the pack had left him to his own devices of late, that was a worry he could put away in the back of his mind. The immediate situation was easily resolved. These men, like Jonathan and Roger, had gotten into the business of rum-running to make money.

He couldn't replace the jug of hooch that Roger and Jonathan had opened, but money was something of which he had plenty. And he'd fortunately put on the trousers containing the wallet he'd brought into town the day before, which still contained plenty of cash despite what he'd spent at the grocer's.

"Our customers are expecting a full shipment," Hugh said. "They're already upset it's running late." He looked sad as he added, "They are kids. Not much older than mine, by the look. But we're not the only ones in the business here, and it's not our say what happens to those who cross the bigger fish."

Malachi pulled out his wallet. "Tell you what. You say what it'll take to get the heat off those boys, and I'll pay it."

"Why do you care?" The nameless man squinted at him suspiciously. "You hiding them in there? Maybe we should have Tanner take a look."

"If you try to enter my home without my consent, it won't go well." Malachi bared his teeth in what might have passed as a smile. The other man's face paled again. "I'll give you enough so you can take a cut before you send some on to your customers. Consider it an apology for the short shipment."

"You were at school with my sister." Hugh looked closely at Malachi. "Sheila Corkum, you remember her?"

"I do." He had taken her out once or twice during their last years at the town's academy, which provided education for all grade levels.

"I worked for your father for a while, too. He was a good man." Hugh looked at the other man. "He's all right. Take the offer. Don't know why he's so set on protecting those boys, but if he wants to cover their debt, let him. Tell them we'll pay them triple for the missing jug and we'll make it up on the next shipment."

"They won't like it," the other man said.

"They will when they see the cash." Hugh turned back to Malachi. "A hundred. Twenty each for him and me, sixty for the customer."

"Done." That would take nearly all of what Malachi had on hand, and he would still need to pay off Jonathan's debtors, but he had more squirreled away. And it would be worth it to free Jonathan and Roger from always looking over their shoulders, wondering whether the rumrunners were pursuing them. Bad enough he would still have to guard against the possibility of the other wolves finding him. He didn't need the added worry about humans returning to his territory to take Jonathan and Roger from him.

He took out five twenty-dollar bills and handed them to Hugh, whom he trusted more than the other man. Hugh pocketed the money without bothering to count it. "If you happen to see those boys, you tell them they're out of the bootlegging business for good. If they try to get back into it, I'm not responsible for what happens to them. Money or not, some people won't be happy about this. They'll do best to lay low and stay out of sight of those people."

"I'll be sure to pass along the message if I see them," Malachi replied.

Hugh nodded. "Come on, Fred. We'll let Pat know the problem's solved."

The other man opened and closed his mouth, evidently unable to decide whether to argue or accept the turn in events.

Finally he spun around without a word and stalked off toward the neighboring cottage.

"I'll make sure you're left alone," Hugh said. "Sheila always spoke well of you. You don't have to hide out here, you know."

"Something happened at university," Malachi replied. "I lost someone close to me. And then my parents last year. I prefer being alone now."

Hugh nodded, sympathy in his eyes. "I understand. Just know you still have friends in town. Take care." He strode away after his colleague.

Malachi watched them climb the wooden beams that acted as steps upward to the gravel road that led away from the cottage. Once they were out of sight, he closed the door and sighed. He'd gotten them away from his men. More, Hugh's statement reassured him. Humans might not be much of a match for werewolves, but if the pack ever found him, at least he'd have someone to go to for help.

As long as it had been since the last time he'd seen the pack, he began to wonder whether they intended to find him. Perhaps they'd stopped looking. But it was still good to know he wouldn't be alone if they came.

A soft gasp came from the bedroom, followed by a louder moan. "Hush," Roger whispered harshly. "He'll hear."

"Can't help it," Jonathan said. "Feels too good."

"It'll be like on the beach," Roger said in a teasing tone. "He'll hear and he'll come in and watch and then he'll join. You want that, Jonny? You want to fuck with just me, or you want Malachi here too?"

Malachi leaned against the front door, desire filling him again. He knew what he wanted, and this time he wouldn't be ashamed of the yearning or of following it through. Roger wanted him. He knew that. But he wouldn't intrude on them uninvited. Not again. Half-aware, he cupped his hardening prick with one hand and waited for Jonathan's answer.

"I like Malachi," Jonathan said slowly. "I like you, too. Not quite the same way, because I've known you longer, but it's almost the same. Is that wrong?"

Malachi's heart soared. He didn't know whether the younger man was talking about love or only physical desire, but it didn't matter. Jonathan had some affection for him, which made him feel considerably less stupid about his own feelings. Feelings that hadn't had time yet to fully form, but he hoped they would. If Jonathan and Roger agreed to stay.

Roger chuckled. "You're asking me if it's wrong that you want to fuck us both? Or if it's wrong that you care about us both?"

"I don't know."

"Neither one's wrong, Jonny." Roger's voice took on a tender note. "Nothing's wrong about anything as long as everyone agrees. As long as everyone's old enough and has wits enough to say yes or no, and we all are, right?"

"Right." The bed creaked. "We're talking too much."

"You started it." Another gasp from Jonathan punctuated Roger's words. "Don't worry, Jonny. I'm going to fuck you. I want you so much it hurts. But I'm playing smart here. He's going to hear us. For all we know, he's standing out there listening right now."

Startled, Malachi felt his face heat. He was eavesdropping, and the fact that Roger knew it bothered him, though not as much as it ought to have.

"He was good to me after—on the beach," Jonathan said. "I don't mind if he hears."

"And if I say I want him to join us?"

Guilt took over Malachi's arousal, and his cock softened. *This isn't right.* He was lurking in his own home, waiting for an invitation he had no right to anticipate, listening to what should have been a private conversation between lovers. In an attempt to drown out the men's voices, he started washing the dishes from the night before.

"He's in the kitchen." Roger's voice was barely covered by the running water and the clanging of dishes against the metal sink.

"You said you're mine," Jonathan said.

"Meant it, too." The bed creaked again. "Long as you want me to be. If it's just you and me, okay. It doesn't have to be just us, though, if we both say it doesn't. At least not in bed."

"People do that?"

Roger laughed. "What do you think we did on the beach?"

"I mean all the time. That just happened. People plan it?"

"I don't know about people. I just know about us." Roger paused. Malachi started washing a plate he'd already cleaned just to have a reason to keep the water running. He should have just left the cottage when he'd heard that first moan from Jonathan. The younger men should have had privacy for this discussion instead of having a lonely werewolf hanging on every word.

"You keep touching me there, I can't think enough to decide nothing," Jonathan said.

"Sorry. Your cock's so pretty, I can't help touching it. Touch me, too." Roger made a pleased sound. "That's the way. You can touch me anywhere you like, Jonny."

"Can he?" Jonathan's words came faster. "Can Malachi touch you anywhere too? Do you want him to? Do you want to touch him?"

"Too many questions." Now Roger moaned. "God, Jonny, so good!"

"Malachi, come in here," Jonathan called.

Malachi wanted to refuse. The man was only calling him out of lust, out of a wish to end the discussion with Roger. But he shut off the water and walked to the bedroom, his entire body tingling in anticipation.

He opened the door slowly and was treated to the lovely sight of two nude men entwined on the bed. Roger's hand was between Jonathan's legs, cupping his balls. Anticipation grew to hunger, and Malachi ached to put his hands on the men's bare skin and have them caress him. His prick grew hard again, and at the thought of either Jonathan's or Roger's mouth on his shaft, he closed his eyes and sighed.

Then he abruptly opened his eyes again. He'd been invited in, but he refused to make assumptions.

Jonathan was smiling at him, looking past Roger. "You were listening."

"I couldn't help it." Malachi's face heated again. "I hear better than humans. I would have had to go outdoors to keep from hearing you."

Jonathan wrapped his hand around Roger's shaft. Roger moaned and looked over his shoulder at Malachi. Malachi shivered at the sheer eroticism of the sight. Even if they sent him away now, this vision would fill his fantasies for years.

"He wants you," Jonathan said. "I don't know nothing about it except what we did on the beach, but just now Roger's been showing me how good all this feels."

"Taking it slow," Roger said. He gasped as Jonathan squeezed him. "Not so rough, Jonny. Too much. Do it slow. Like I should have taken you the first time."

Jonathan kissed Roger's shoulder and looked surprised at himself for it. "First time, you were slow. It hurt, but I still liked it. Liked having you in me." He looked at Malachi. "He liked what you did, too. And you like seeing us like this?"

"Yes." The word came out harshly, and Malachi took a deep breath. Lust brought the wolf. On the beach, sheer luck had kept him from hurting Roger. He wouldn't make that mistake again.

For a moment, Jonathan looked uncertain. This was all new to him. Malachi nearly left the room, knowing that as long as he stood there, Jonathan might feel obliged to agree to Roger's suggestion. If he left, they could have their time together, as they deserved.

"There's room for three," Jonathan said finally, his voice rising in pitch. "I mean, if you want to."

"Jonny, be sure," Roger said. He pulled away from his lover and stood beside the bed. "I love you. I was wrong the other day. Pushed you too hard. I won't do it again. I'll go without for the rest of my life if you have any doubt at all."

"You weren't pushing me just now." Jonathan sat up, confusion and dejection warring in his expression. "Pete's sakes, Roger, do you think I didn't like that? Being so close to you, how could I help liking it?" He paused. "I love you too. And I wanted to be pushed the other day, because I was too damn scared to do it any other way." He looked at Malachi. "I don't know how to say this, but it feels like it shouldn't be just him and me. Not all the time, anyway. Like you were there the first time, and you should be here now."

Malachi pressed his lips together and looked at the floor, trying to hide the emotion which flooded him. He understood what Jonathan was trying to say. After over a decade of being alone, of belonging nowhere and to no one, these two men who had come to him purely by chance wanted him with them. If he looked either of them in the eye now, he might be overcome, and that was something he refused to permit at a time like this.

"Be sure," Roger said again. "You know what I want."

"That isn't why I'm saying yes," Jonathan said. "It's because I think you're right. I barely know how it works with two, never mind three, but we can sort it out."

"Yeah, and it'll be fun sorting it." Roger touched Malachi's hand. "You heard us before you came in and you hear what he's saying now. You want it?"

"Yes." Malachi looked up, though he still couldn't meet either man's eyes.

"No more talking, then." Roger gave him the same mischievous grin as the day before. "Can't fuck you if you got clothes on. Take them off and get on here with us."

He got back onto the bed and flicked his tongue against one of Jonathan's nipples. Jonathan arched his back and sighed. Malachi unfastened his trousers while he watched Roger lick and kiss down Jonathan's torso to the blond man's hard shaft. As Malachi dropped his trousers to the floor, Roger slid his lips down Jonathan's prick, and Jonathan gasped and looked into Malachi's eyes.

Malachi gave up any resistance or doubt. He stepped out of

his trousers and knelt on the bed, caressing Roger's ass while the man sucked his lover.

Roger took his mouth off Jonathan long enough to say, "Fuck me. Wet up and fuck me."

The bed was barely large enough, but somehow they managed to find positions that allowed what they all wanted. Malachi used his wet fingers to stretch Roger's hole, and just feeling that heat and tightness on his fingers sent his desire spiraling. Jonathan cried out and bucked beneath Roger. "Oh, fuck!"

"Didn't think you'd come so fast." Roger looked back at Malachi. "Wanted you in me while I sucked him, but do it anyway. Please."

"I want to see." Jonathan sat up slightly and took hold of Roger's cock. "Should I do this while he fucks you?"

"Yes," Roger gasped.

"Thought you said no more talking." Malachi crooked a finger at Jonathan. "Remember how you got him ready to fuck you? Do that to me."

Jonathan's eyes lit up and he squirmed out from below Roger to take Malachi's cock in his mouth. He was far from expert, but the slick wetness of his lips and tongue felt wonderful. Malachi's head lolled back and he closed his eyes, letting the younger man stoke his hunger. He forced himself to keep control. His wolf rose as his lust did, and he was close to spending before more than a few moments had passed.

"Stop," he gasped when the pleasure became too much to bear. "Do it to him now."

Jonathan moved again and ran his tongue over the tip of Roger's cock. Roger moaned and arched his back, and Malachi took the opportunity to begin pressing his prick forward into the man's tight hole. Roger cried out wordlessly as Malachi took him. Malachi forced himself to be easy, not wanting to hurt Roger no matter how desperate he was to feel that tightness around his cock.

Jonathan looked up at Malachi and smiled. He might have

been uncertain how to proceed, but he seemed to have no objections to what was going on. Seeing the lust in the younger man's eyes fueled Malachi's own, and he pushed forward one last time, fully penetrating Roger.

"God, yes," Roger murmured.

Malachi wanted to stay like that, savoring the sensation of being inside the man, but his desire was far too strong. He knew he would last only moments. Jonathan had brought him too close to the breaking point. But he couldn't hold back. He slowly pulled out, then thrust back into Roger's ass, eliciting a gasp from both of them. Jonathan took Roger's cock in his mouth again, and Malachi both smelled and felt the pleasure mounting in his partner and himself.

It was over far too quickly. Malachi's climax took him by surprise. He realized it was coming too late to stop it. Frantically, he thrust again and again into his partner, hoping to bring Roger off before he spent. He didn't succeed. His seed erupted from him and the accompanying ecstasy washed all clear thoughts from his mind. Dimly he heard Roger's moan and hoped it meant that Jonathan had finished him.

He closed his eyes as he spasmed again. For just a moment, he felt what Jonathan had mentioned, the sense that the three of them belonged together. Odd as it seemed, in that instant Malachi believed it fully.

When he recovered enough to move, he withdrew from Roger and sprawled on his back at the foot of the bed, breathing heavily. Roger collapsed onto his stomach and craned his neck to look back at Malachi. "Nice."

"Very." Malachi smiled. "Much better than against a rock on the beach."

"Yeah."

Jonathan sat at the head of the bed, looking sated and triumphant. "I didn't mind the rock much."

Roger laughed weakly. "I don't believe you. Come here, would you?"

Jonathan lay beside him, and Roger slung an arm across his

lover's back. The men's affection toward each other made Malachi happy, but he felt left out until Roger reached back with his free hand. "You too."

"Not enough room." Malachi took Roger's hand and tried to pretend his heart hadn't expanded to twice its natural size.

They lay together in companionable silence for long minutes. Malachi thought Roger might have fallen asleep for a time; his breathing slowed and deepened. He nearly slept himself, content to be with these men even if it might not last.

"Who was at the door?" Jonathan asked finally.

Malachi started. He must have been closer to sleep than he'd realized. "As you thought. Two of the rumrunners, along with a police officer."

"Cops?" Roger rolled off the bed and stood staring down at Malachi. "Cops were here and you didn't say nothing? I knew about the runners. Jonny told me. That's why—I wanted to distract him so he wasn't so scared."

"They were gone before I heard you," Malachi replied. "I sent the officer to check one of the other cottages and meanwhile persuaded the rumrunners to leave you both alone."

"You didn't turn wolf again, did you?" Roger took a deep breath. "That would have scared them half to death, I bet."

"Probably, but no, I didn't." Malachi sat up and looked around for something to cover himself with. Despite the discussion, seeing Roger standing nude before him had Malachi's cock responding again. He would need to learn better control if the men agreed to stay. "Money can be far more persuasive than fear."

"You bought them off?" Jonathan asked.

"Yes, and I'll buy off the men you owe, too, if you want." Malachi looked at Roger again. "I told you that."

Roger scowled. "We ain't after your money. Didn't we show that already?"

"You aren't asking. I'm offering. And I paid the rumrunners without your knowledge." Malachi gave up the search. His trousers were on the floor behind Roger; he would get them when they were finished talking. “It isn’t charity, and you aren’t taking anything I’m not willing to give.”

“I don’t want to be scared anymore.” Jonathan rummaged among the bedclothes and pulled out the trousers he’d worn the night before. He shimmied into them, still sitting on the bed. “We can work to pay you back. I don’t think you’ll ask for double or more than what you’ve lent.”

“It isn’t a loan, but you can pay it off if you like.” Malachi took a deep breath. He wanted to ask them—to *beg* them—to stay, but he couldn’t. Not yet. “We’ll talk more after we clean up. And cook. We should eat.”

“You’re stalling.” Roger turned and bent elaborately, exposing himself to Jonathan and Malachi. Malachi’s cock stirred and he closed his eyes to keep himself from becoming too aroused again. Roger chuckled and something landed on Malachi’s legs. “Put those on if you’re ashamed of what we’re seeing. You shouldn’t be. It’s too nice to be ashamed of.”

Malachi opened his eyes to see Roger’s gaze fixed obviously on Malachi’s cock. “I’m not ashamed. There’s a time and place, and we’ve had our time this morning.” He stood and turned Roger toward the door. “The two of you can use the washroom. Go on.”

Roger opened his mouth, doubtless to tease Malachi again. Jonathan put his hand over Roger’s mouth. “Stop it and come with me.”

Roger held up his hands in surrender and followed Jonathan out of the room. Malachi shook his head, smiling. They would be entertaining to have around, no question.

He cleaned himself at the kitchen sink, using cold water that helped to quell what Roger had tried to start. When the other two emerged from the washroom, both clothed, Malachi was standing in trousers and shirt at the stove, frying bread and apple slices. “How long are you staying?”

“Through breakfast, at least.” Roger took down three plates. “We didn’t get paid, so I don’t have the money I planned to use to get us out west."

"I could give you that, too." Malachi's heart sank. They were still planning to leave, by the sound. He didn't want to offer them the means to do so, but he wouldn't keep them here if they didn't want to stay.

"That isn't what I mean." Roger put his hand on Malachi's shoulder. "You and I talked yesterday, and Jonny and I talked just now. You said we could stay, him and me."

"Yes," Malachi said, unwilling to let himself hope for too much.

"We want to," Jonathan said. "I don't like Halifax. Too dangerous. Can't get much safer than living with a werewolf, I guess."

"Except at the full moon." Roger paused. "Is that true?"

"I have to change at the full moon, yes." Malachi picked up the shaker of cinnamon from the shelf above the stove and sprinkled some into the frying pan. "I'd go away from you when that happens. I don't want to know what it would be like to change inside. I'd be out in the woods until it was over, so you'd be safe from me."

"Why do you live alone here?" Jonathan asked. "Don't werewolves have packs, or is that just real wolves?"

"Werewolves do. I don't." Malachi bit his lip. "It's a long story. I'd rather not go into it right now." The two men had shared enough about their lives with him, but he couldn't bring himself to tell them what had happened with the pack. Not yet. "I'm alone because I wanted to be."

"And now?" Roger said.

"Now I have two men who showed up on my beach and got stuck in my mind." Malachi hesitated, then decided he had nothing to lose. "And in my heart. I'm tired of being alone, and I'd be happy to have you if you want to stay."

"I already said." Jonathan leaned against the wall beside the stove. "Feels like it ought to be three of us, not just me and Roger. Except sometimes." He gave Roger a fond smile. "Sometimes I like being alone with you."

"We have our own room," Roger pointed out. "Three's fun sometimes too, though." He grinned at Malachi before turning to Jonathan. "As long as everyone agrees. Told you I'm yours."

"You're mine, I'm yours, we're both his, he's both of ours." Jonathan laughed. "Sounds odder out loud than in my head. I agree, Roger, if you didn't guess by what we were doing a little bit ago. If we ask Malachi to join in, that's okay with me." He looked thoughtful. "And I guess if you or I want to be alone with him...?"

"We can. Or we can figure it out as we go." Roger embraced the younger man. "That's how it works, Jonny. We figure it out as we go. Right now I'm too hungry to figure out anything more than putting food in my mouth."

Malachi smiled, his heart rising again. But he had to hear it straight out before he would allow himself to believe it. He'd been alone too long to take anything for granted. "You're staying?"

"We're staying." Roger reached out to include Malachi in the embrace.

Malachi set down the spatula and allowed himself to be pulled into the other men's arms. He closed his eyes and breathed in their scent. Such a strong emotion rose in him that he nearly wept, but he kept that to himself. Love didn't happen overnight, and he didn't know whether he wanted love in his life. For now, he knew only that he cared for these men, and they for him. And that was enough.

Keep up with the northeastern werewolves! Scan the QR code to join my mailing list and get updates and access to exclusive content.

Malachi returns in the present day and meets his true mate in

EBB AND FLOW

(Ebb & Flow 1)

Scan the QR code to go to the book's sale page, and read on for a short excerpt!

THE SUN was red as it rose over the bay. *Red sky in the morning, sailor take warning.*

Through the picture window in the main room of my cottage, I had a perfect view of the sunrise. Every morning, I made a point of getting up to watch it. Every morning, I remembered how much Jonathan had loved to do the same. Roger had always teased him for it, but Jonathan loved that sunrise. And Roger loved Jonathan.

And I loved both of them. Even though they were long dead.

I didn't watch the sunrise for my own sake. After over a century of life, I'd seen too many. I watched them for Jonathan. They were the only thing I had left of him.

But this morning, the memories of Jonathan and Roger were dulled by a sense of foreboding. Nothing I could put my finger on. Only that something was coming my way and I would do well to avoid it. *Red sky in the morning, sailor take warning.*

When the sun was high enough that the red-tinged clouds gave way to blue sky, I went into the kitchen to boil water for my coffee. Filling the same kettle my mother had used throughout my childhood, over a century earlier, I tuned into what was going on outdoors. It was high summer. Most of the cottages around mine were occupied right now. Which meant I stayed inside most of the time. The last thing I needed was the summer folk marveling at how I never seemed any older. Werewolves aged far more slowly than humans. And humans couldn't know werewolves existed.

Roger and Jonathan had known. I wasn't part of a pack. Hadn't had an Alpha telling me what I was and wasn't allowed to say. So I told them. I knew the rules, of course, but Jonathan and Roger were something special. They'd rated the truth. And so far as I knew, they'd never told anyone else. Even after I sent them away, they'd kept my confidence.

Outside, the sounds of people starting their day mingled with the cries of gulls and crows and the lapping of the waves against the shore. The tide was coming in, which meant it was close on time for me to head out in my boat if I intended to get out at all. I could go at low tide, but high tide made getting the rowboat off the beach easier. And a rowboat was all I had. My parents had left me the cottage in their will, but their boat had gone to one of my sisters. I could have bought a new one. Gods knew I'd squirreled away enough cash over the years. But I liked the rowboat. The physical labor of getting myself from one place to another soothed me.

First, coffee. Breakfast, too. Eggs and sausage. The same thing I'd eaten nearly every morning for as long as I could remember. The same routine every morning. Rise before dawn, clean up, get dressed. Watch the sunrise, or watch the sky lighten if clouds obscured the sun. Coffee and breakfast. Then settle in with a book or a painting if I chose to stay home, or head out to stock up on supplies.

After so many years, I was damn tired of the same old same old. But at the same time, I counted on it. I didn't know how to change.

When I finally left the house, the sun was dancing lights across the water of the bay. A few of the neighbors were down on the shore when I headed down, and I nodded to them but didn't speak. They didn't either. They were accustomed to greeting me in silence by now. Not an unfriendly silence, just respect for the "hermit," as I was known. I bent over my boat and started undoing the lines securing it to a tree at the edge of the sand.

"Malachi Powers."

I started at hearing my name spoken by an unfamiliar voice but hid my reaction. Few people around here knew me. Meaning this was likely not a person, something my instincts confirmed. Another werewolf. Not a friend. Not necessarily an enemy either, though; that remained to be seen.

"I'm Malachi. How can I help you?" I didn't turn around, and I kept my voice low. The humans were too near for comfort, and I had to make sure they didn't notice anything until I ascertained whether this visitor was a threat.

"Come with me, please," he said, matching my volume. "I'm here on behalf of someone who would like to meet with you."

"I have things to do. I don't have time to meet with someone who can't bother to contact me himself." Now I straightened and turned, ready to fight if need be. The man behind me was young, his face half-hidden by thick brown hair matching what grew too long from his head.

He held up both hands. "I'm just delivering a message. Please come with me. My car's up on the main road."

That explained why I hadn't heard an engine or car door. However, I didn't have an answer as to why I hadn't noticed the man following me down to the beach, or, for that matter, why he hadn't confronted me outside the cottage instead of letting me get this far. To the beach from which I could easily escape. My boat was untied and ready to go.

He gestured toward a trio of children taking tentative steps into the water nearby. "It would be easier if you came with me."

My chest tightened, and I tensed, unsure whether to run or fight to defend my neighbors. Threatening humans? Perhaps that was why he'd followed me to the beach. So he would have leverage against me.

The threat left me little choice. I couldn't risk anything happening to the people among whom I made my home. Especially the children.

"Let me tie the boat again," I said. "I'll lose it otherwise."

"Go ahead." The man folded his arms.

I retied the lines, paying no mind to the curious looks of the children and the few adults scattered around the beach. One of them, Cilla Creighton from the cottage next to mine, approached but stopped a couple of meters away. "Everything all right, Malachi?"

"Yes, Cilla, it's fine." *Go away*. I'd known Cilla since she was a child. Hell, I'd known her grandfather as a child. Of all the humans around here, she was the last one I wanted to see anything happen to. "Just some business to attend to. Have a nice day."

"You too." She looked puzzled but asked nothing more, to my relief.

I motioned toward the wooden stairs that led from the beach up to my cottage. My visitor nodded. "After you."

Not trusting me at his back. Probably wise. I wouldn't attack, but he had no way to know that. Wouldn't run, either, since I doubted I could outrun him, but he didn't know that either. I dipped my head toward Cilla and headed up the stairs.

The man stayed behind me all the way out to the main road, where a large gray SUV waited on the shoulder. He went to the passenger door and opened it. "Get in."

"Not until you tell me who you are and who sent you." I waved toward the trees that lined the road. "No humans here. Speak freely."

He scoffed. "I don't need your permission, packless. Get in."

"I said no." Times like this, I almost wished I'd given in and stayed part of Mahone Bay Pack after my change. Not that I'd had a whole lot of times like this, but it would have been good to have others at my back. "Who are you, and who sent you?"

"I can force you into this damn car."

"You can't, or you already would have." Which begged the question, why hadn't he? Someone had sent him to get me. Someone he took orders from, who probably wouldn't be too happy if I didn't arrive as commanded.

Unless they were already here.

Too late, I heard the rustling in the brush beside me. Two

men lunged out of the trees and grabbed my arms. Without a word, they shoved me into the back seat of the vehicle. One got into the front passenger seat, the other into the driver's. My original visitor got into the back beside me.

We drove to the highway and headed north. None of them said anything, so I didn't either. I had nothing to say.

Would anyone even notice I was gone? Besides Cilla and maybe a handful of my other neighbors, probably not. For that matter, I took off from time to time, so even my neighbors were likely to think nothing of me being gone for a few days. No other wolves would.

None except Silas, who after a while might wonder why I hadn't shown up at his island compound to harass him. And my mate, but since I generally avoided contact with him, maybe he wouldn't be aware anything had happened to me.

My mate. A man, which had stunned me. I'd been told mated pairs were always of the opposite sex. I had no problem with him being a man. Actually preferred it. His age, though… that was another story. He barely looked grown. Not much older than Roger and Jonathan were when I met them. Back then, when I was barely past thirty myself, being with men a decade or so younger than me had felt awkward but acceptable.

But over Quinn, who'd told me he was twenty-two, I had more than a century. He had his whole life ahead of him, and it would be a long life. Most of my life was behind me. And I still grieved for Jonathan and Roger, despite how long they'd been gone.

Quinn was grieving too. Only days before we met, he'd lost his lover and nearly half his pack to an attack by a neighboring pack. He wasn't ready for a mate. Even if I'd been willing to accept him, it wouldn't have been right. And I wasn't about to accept some foolish fated bond to a boy who needed far more than I'd be able to give him.

At the moment, it was irrelevant anyway. The thoughts were a welcome distraction from my current circumstances, but they didn't change the fact that I didn't know whether I was going to see my cottage again, never mind my mate.

We exited the highway near Halifax and headed west. In a rural area, surrounded by fields and trees, the SUV stopped.

"Get out," the man beside me said.

I didn't bother with any opposition this time. Three of them, one of me, and all of us wolves weren't odds I wanted to gamble. I opened the door and stepped out. Soon as the door was closed, the vehicle took off.

Leaving me standing in the woods in a part of the province I knew well. Not as well as Lunenburg and Herman's Island, but well enough I could easily find my way home from here. Particularly with no one stopping me. What in Hades was going on here?

Another car pulled to a stop. A tall, stoop-shouldered man got out of the passenger side. Him, I recognized. "Esau."

"Malachi." Esau Walters, Alpha of Annapolis Valley Pack, closed the car door and strode toward me. The first time I'd met the man, on one of my visits to Silas, the dislike had been instant and mutual. "We need to talk."

"I'd say we do." I couldn't believe he had condoned his men threatening humans. Anyone else, I would have given the benefit of the doubt and considered that perhaps they hadn't known the lengths their henchmen would go to, but Esau was the kind that didn't care who was in harm's way so long as he got what he wanted. "Your goons brought me here. What do you want?"

"To offer you an alliance." He paused. "You're friendly with the Anax."

"I am." Immediately, I was on guard. Silas Creighton had attained the rank of Anax through fighting and skill, and he'd held it by proving himself a fair ruler. But not everyone was in favor of him, particularly now since he'd brokered peace with the Anax of the United States. None had challenged him to a fair fight for rank, and I suspected none would. They knew they couldn't win. Instead, they would rather manipulate and ambush, as they'd done only weeks earlier.

The men who had attempted to end the life of the American

Anax during his visit had nearly killed my mate. They were fortunate they'd died before I could take action against them.

My only reason for suspecting Esau of having malicious intent was my distaste for the man, but that was reason enough. I'd yet to question my instincts about people, and I wasn't starting now.

"There are those who'd like to see someone else in that rank," he said.

"I am aware." A pang in my side reminded me of how aware. And of who that pain actually belonged to. I wasn't the one who'd been shot.

Now wasn't a time for dwelling. Or thinking about the skinny, light-haired boy who apparently was destined to be mine for life.

"We want your help." Esau clasped his hands in front of him. "You have the Anax's trust."

"I do," I said. "And I will not betray it."

Before he could speak, I took my wolf form. Shifting, for most, was a long, painful process. For me, it was nearly instant, though it hurt like hell and destroyed the clothes I hadn't had time to remove. Ignoring the pain, and not caring about the clothes, I ran.

The men who'd brought me were nowhere in sight. Esau was but, still in human form, he couldn't catch me. Nor could he if he took the time to shift, since it would take him considerably longer than it had taken me. I would have a head start.

The question was where to go. I wanted to be back in my cottage. There, generally, I was safe. Today, though, I wouldn't be. Esau and his men would expect me to return home. If I did, they would only find me again, and the humans in the other cottages would be at greater risk.

By land, the dock nearest Silas's compound was quite a few kilometers from here. But it was closer and safer than home, and as a wolf, I could run it. Even in my old age, in wolf form, I didn't tire easily. I ran, hoping the alarm hadn't been sounded. Hoping Esau and his men wouldn't find me.

And they did not. Through woods and along barely traveled

roads, I ran, ducking away from passing cars. Any human who saw me now might believe me to be a genuine wolf, but I would still draw attention. Wolves were far from common in Nova Scotia.

Finally, I neared my goal. Of course, I couldn't run all the way to Silas's compound. Walking—or running—on water wasn't within my power, and the mass of a werewolf's wolf-form body didn't permit swimming or floating. If I entered the water, I would sink. All I could do was hope Silas or his men had left a boat tied to the shoreside dock.

Providence was in my favor. Although the power boat Silas kept for transporting himself and his men across the narrow channel between the mainland and his island wasn't there, a dinghy was tied to the small wooden dock at the edge of the water. A quick glance around assured me no humans were near, nor, as far as I could tell, were any enemies. I took a breath and shifted back into my human form.

Again pushing away my awareness of the pain from shifting, I cast off the dinghy's line and jumped in as it started to float away.

One of Silas's men met me on the island's dock, where the power boat was tied. "Malachi."

"Wallace." I tossed him the line. He tied the dinghy off, then threw me a pair of shorts. I stepped onto the dock and pulled them on. "Silas around?"

"He's here." Wallace nodded toward the house. "Is something wrong? You don't usually show up unannounced." He let out a quiet chuckle. "Or unclothed."

"I'd prefer to talk to Silas directly.," I said, choosing to ignore his last comment. "Do I need an escort?"

Wallace shook his head and took his phone out of his pocket. He tapped on the screen. "Silas trusts you. I'm just texting the house to let them know you're on the way up." The phone made a chirping sound, and he glanced at it. "Go ahead."

"Thanks."

When I reached the house, a short distance across an

expanse of grass, Silas and another of his men were waiting on the porch. Silas held his hands out to his sides. "Malachi Powers, packless wolf, you are welcome in my home. May no harm come to you here."

I had no idea why he'd chosen to stand on ceremony, but I knew the expected response. "Silas Creighton, Anax of Canada, I thank you for your hospitality. May I bring no harm to your home."

He grinned and extended a hand, which I shook. "Old friend. You always look so uncomfortable when you answer my greeting."

"Ah, so you did it so you could laugh at me." I gave him a small smile. "In this case, the greeting was warranted. This isn't a social call."

"I thought not." He sighed. "Come in. Tell me what happened. And why you've come here instead of phoning."

Right. A cell phone. I had one of those, which I rarely used. My cottage still had the corded wall phone I'd installed decades ago, which served for the few calls I needed to make. The cell phone was to allow me to keep in touch with Quinn. For that reason, I tended to forget I had it and never brought it with me when I left the cottage.

Not that it would have helped in this instance. As a wolf, I wouldn't have been able to carry the damn thing.

"Didn't think of it," I said.

He shook his head. "Of course not. Come with me."

I followed him into the house, his man trailing. Inside, Silas didn't bother with the formality of bringing me into his office. Instead, we went to the dining room, where two plates were set with battered chicken pieces, mashed potatoes, and corn. The food smelled divine.

"Hungry?" Silas said as he sat at the head of the table.

"You knew I was coming." I sat to his right. His man stayed in the doorway.

"Packless or not, you're one of my wolves. My bond to all

wolves in Canada includes you." He picked up his fork but didn't eat. "You could have called me for help. I don't mean by phone."

"I was all right." I was also starving. Two shifts and running however many kilometers had worked up an appetite.

I picked up a piece of chicken and tore off a chunk with my teeth. It was delicious. Silas had an incredible cook working for him.

"You weren't all right," he said. "Tell me what happened, Malachi."

I chewed and swallowed while he sat and watched. "I was heading out for supplies," I said when my mouth was empty. "Someone met me on the beach. There were humans down there. Children. My, let's say visitor, made it clear that if I chose not to go with him, something would happen to those people."

Silas narrowed his eyes. "He threatened humans?"

"Yes. Humans amongst whom I live in the summer." I tore off another bite of chicken.

"Who was he?"

I chewed and swallowed. "I'm not sure. But he brought me to Esau Walters."

"Esau?" Silas's voice went up.

"I can't say for sure that he knew about the threats." I was fairly certain of it, but I refused to say what I couldn't prove. "He was the one who ordered me taken to him, though. No question about that. They dropped me off in the middle of nowhere, and there he was."

"For what purpose?"

Those who didn't know Silas well might have missed the note of quiet fury in his voice. I'd known him since we were boys, years before either of us was changed. He was barely containing his anger. Not only because of the danger to the humans, but the threat to me as well.

He would be angrier in a moment.

"He informed me that there are some who would prefer to see a new Anax." I put down the chicken. "Since it's known that I have your trust, he thought I might assist with your removal."

It didn't take a bond to feel the rage emanating from him. An understandable reaction. Not many would have taken such news well. Still, when he spoke, his voice was quiet. "There's a conspiracy against me. Old news, but now we have a new name on the list."

"We do." I picked up the chicken again. Angry Anax or not, I needed to eat. And Silas's anger didn't frighten me. "I don't know who else might be involved. I don't think the wolves he sent to collect me were of his pack, though I can't know for sure."

"I'll find out." He let out a long breath and picked up his fork. "Thank you for coming to me with this, Malachi. You didn't only come to inform me, though, did you?"

"If I return home, they'll likely look for me there again." I took a smaller bite of the chicken than the previous ones and swallowed it quickly. "If it was winter, it wouldn't matter. No humans around me then. But at this time of year, all the cottages are occupied. I didn't want to take the risk."

"Wise thinking. Unfortunately, they may go there looking for you, and your absence doesn't preclude them taking action against the humans." Silas stood. I couldn't judge whether banging his fist on the table was intentional or not. "Tavish!"

"Yes, Anax." Wherever Tavish was, it took him only seconds to reach the dining room.

"Esau Walters is to be brought here. I'd like you and Angus to handle it." He looked toward the door through which we'd entered, which was actually the back of the house. The front faced the open water. "You'll go once our guest arrives, which should be momentarily."

"Yes, Anax." Tavish didn't move. Well trained, it seemed.

"Please go let Angus know, and alert Wallace and Stanton that I'll need them here while you're gone. The mainland side will have to be unattended until you come back."

"That should only be a couple of hours, Anax," Tavish said. "I'll let them know."

"Thank you." Silas gave a curt nod. "Go ahead."

Tavish left, and Silas sat down again. “We’ll see what Esau has to say for himself.”

“Guest?” I asked.

“Esau won’t be a guest.” He looked at me grimly.

“No, fool.” I shook my head. “You told Tavish to go after Esau once your guest arrives. What guest might that be?”

The whine of a plane engine stopped Silas from answering, or perhaps he hadn’t intended to answer. “Finish your meal,” he said instead. “You’ll see in a few minutes.”

The whine grew louder, drilling a hole through my skull. My childhood had occurred in a time without planes, but by the time I was grown, they’d existed. I should have been used to them by now, but it seemed like the damn things proliferated and got louder every year. I hated the noise. One of the better things about Herman’s Island was its distance from any flight paths.

Not that Silas’s island was on flight paths in general. However, it had its own airstrip. Silas, for that matter, had his own plane, albeit one he seldom used. The approaching aircraft had to be the guest he’d mentioned.

I gulped down the rest of my chicken and some of the potatoes before the engine’s volume became unbearable. Knowing my hatred of the noise, Silas said nothing when I pushed my plate away and covered my ears. A childish act, and one which did little to dull the noise, but it deceived my brain into thinking things had gotten at least a bit quieter.

Finally, the sound cut off. Silas stood and nodded toward the door. “Let’s go greet the guest.”

Something in his tone hinted that this wasn’t any typical guest. Not that there was such a thing among werewolves, particularly werewolves who traveled by private plane. However, the visitors who usually arrived by plane were the arkhons, the regional leaders, who came to meet with Silas for business or during the once-yearly gathering he held to assess the state of werewolfery in Canada. This year’s meeting had come and gone in early June, well over a month prior, so this was likely business.

Or so I would have believed if not for that note in his voice and the look on his face.

“What are you on about?” I asked.

He didn’t answer, just walked up the hall and out the back door as I trailed him, annoyed at his crypticness and at not having finished my meal.

The plane had come to a stop at the nearer end of the runway. As Silas and I approached, a man I didn’t recognize exited, followed by a man I knew.

A man my heart reached toward even though I tried to rein it in.

My mate was here. Quinn.

Author of:

The REAL WEREWOLVES DON'T EAT MEAT series

The EBB & FLOW series

Other male/male paranormal romance

For a complete list, visit

HTTPS://KARENNACOLCROFT.COM/BOOKS/

ABOUT THE AUTHOR

Karenna Colcroft lives just north of Boston, Massachusetts, and has been in love with the city since childhood. To the best of her knowledge, she has yet to encounter any werewolves or other paranormal beings here.

Karenna is a polyamorous, nonbinary human. She lives with her husband and has two adult children and three "bonus" kids, four grandchildren, and three cats, who aren't at all pleased that Karenna writes about werewolves.

Find out more about Karenna online at http://www.karennacolcroft.com or https://www.facebook.com/KarennaColcroft.

Receive a free story and get updates and sneak peeks at Karenna's upcoming books at https://karennacolcroft.com/get-your-free-story/

If you enjoyed this book, please consider leaving a review!

www.ingramcontent.com/pod-product-compliance
Lightning Source LLC
LaVergne TN
LVHW011030110826
845149LV00015B/3357

* 9 7 8 1 9 5 8 3 4 6 3 5 8 *